THE NEXT ICE AGE

Francis A. Andrew

Order this book online at www.trafford.com
or email orders@trafford.com

Most Trafford titles are also available at major online book retailers.

Printed in Victoria, BC, Canada.

ISBN: 978-1-4269-2780-5 (sc)

Library of Congress Control Number: 2010905738

Our mission is to efficiently provide the world's finest, most comprehensive book publishing service, enabling every author to experience success. To find out how to publish your book, your way, and have it available worldwide, visit us online at www.trafford.com

Trafford rev. 7/5/2010

www.trafford.com

North America & international
toll-free: 1 888 232 4444 (USA & Canada)
phone: 250 383 6864 • fax: 812 355 4082

Contents

CHAPTER 1.
The Devil Looks After His own.

The game was up for Adolph Hitler. The Allies were only a few miles from his Berlin bunker and the sound of gunfire and artillery shells could be clearly heard. Their deafening noise told Hitler that it was all over. Martin Bormann advised his Fuhrer that further delay would result in capture. Adolph Hitler nodded in agreement to Bormann.

"Is the Plan ready to be put into operation?" asked the Fuhrer.

"All the details have been meticulously worked out and the first step in its implementation should be taken as soon as possible", Bormann replied.

Bormann left the room and went into his own office. He strolled over to his desk and opened one of the drawers. He slowly but confidently took out a revolver; he put just one bullet into it. He then walked out of the room with the revolver.

In the Fuhrer's living quarters in the bunker, Bormann walked over to the little man with the moustache and asked him to look closely at the revolver. The little man in the moustache did so and Bormann pulled the trigger and blew his head clean away. Bormann then walked through to the main operations room of the bunker.

"Step one of the plan has been completed", said Bormann.

A bald, moustacheless and beardless man who was sitting facing the wall quickly swiveled round and simply stared at Bormann.

"Which look-alike did you use?" the man asked Bormann.

"Number 3. He was the best of the six impersonators."

"Excellent, excellent", replied the hairless man.

"Mein Fuhrer", said Bormann rather nervously, "we must now, with the utmost haste, implement Step 2 of the Great Plan".

"Yes, yes", replied the totally clean-shaven Fuhrer.

Hitler and Bormann walked over to a portion of the office wall. Bormann removed a painting from the wall and laid it carefully on a chair nearby. The painting's removal revealed a single, solitary button. Bormann pressed this button and, as if by magic, two parts of the wall, each about four feet across and eight feet high, parted to reveal a lift. Hitler stepped into the lift and Bormann followed. The doors closed and Hitler and Bormann descended two hundred feet underground. In the main operations room, one of Bormann's minions unscrewed the button and deactivated the lift's mechanism. The wall looked like a wall again, and the doors were sealed forever. The picture was replaced to where it had previously been.

Two hundred feet underground, a long train was waiting for Hitler and Bormann. A staff officer standing erect motioned Hitler and Bormann to one of the compartments.

Once seated in the train compartment, an officer with the rank of colonel came up to Hitler and Bormann. He clicked his heels and gave the Nazi salute.

"Are all 500 of our handpicked Nazi patriots safely ensconced on this train, Colonel Kraner", inquired the Fuhrer.

"They are Mein Fuhrer", replied Colonel Kraner.

"Good. Then let us delay no longer".

Colonel Kraner stepped out of the compartment and motioned to a man who was standing on the platform. The main raised a small flag which he was holding in his hand. In his other hand he held a whistle. He applied the whistle to his lips and soon the train started to move off.

CHAPTER 2.
The Great Court Of Political Correctness.

Judge John Benson sat with a sombre face as he glowered at the court from behind his desk which was situated on a raised dais. He became even more sombre and glowering as he directed his cheerless gaze towards the youth in the dock. Very few people had much to smile about in the year 2037. Britain was now part of a unitary nation called "Europe " and happiness was a scarce commodity. To be more accurate, the 20 regions of what had once been Britain were now ruled directly from Brussels .

"Let the Guilty take the stand", drawled the drab judicial figure.

A youth of around seventeen and a half made his way from the dock to the stand. The look on his face showed him to be at once both proud and angry.

"Are you European Citizen 761 B23 NP46?" the judge asked.

"No I am not!" the youth snapped back.

"How dare you answer in the negative", yelled the clerk of the court. "You must never contradict a judge of Political Correctness".

"Laddie", said Benson, "if I say you are European Citizen 761 B23 NP46, then there can be no two doubts about it that that is exactly who you are".

"My name is Kenneth Mackenzie", snarled the Guilty.

"That is your private and personal name", hollered the judge. "I'll have less of your insubordination. Now what is your address?"

"It is 76, Sir Walter Scott Street , Annan, Dumfries and Galloway ", Mackenzie answered.

Benson banged his clenched fists on his desk. "Are you trying my patience kid? Your address is Citizen House 20, Eurostreet, Mid-Region12".

Mackenzie haughtily looked away from the judge and towards the ceiling of the court.

Mackenzie then spotted his parents who were watching the proceedings from the gallery. The appeal on his mother's face was as if to say "Kenneth, you're our only child, please don't do anything that will get you sent to a re-education camp in some remote corner of Europe ".

"Shall I begin to question the Guilty on the main charge against him, Your Political Correctness?" asked the Politically Correct Prosecutor for Mid-Region 12.

"Yes of course, but before you do that, Mid-Region 12's Religious Enforcer of Politically Correct Doctrine would like to question the citizen first."

A rather dour and wasted looking individual stood up and approached the stand.

"Our Bureau of Religious Affairs has noticed that you have of late been rather lax in your duties towards the Almighty?"

"I am a member of the Church of Scotland and I attend service every Sunday".

"Yes – but when did you last attend a Jean Monett memorial event?"

"I don't see why I should answer any questions when I am not allowed to have a defence counsel".

At this the entire court started to laugh. Even His Political Correctness Judge John Benson let out a guffaw. It was one of those rare occasions when merriment and laughter were permitted. Loudness of laughs was measured by decibel level on European designated sonar style equipment. There were about 20 sizes of smiles and grins that were strictly measured and all categorised by width, length and duration of time. A guidebook had been issued by the European Commissioners on where, when and about what one could show amusement.

When the laughter had died down Benson informed Mackenzie about his 'rights'.

"You are undoubtedly guilty because the High Controller for Politically Correct Matters has said so. No politically correct body can ever be wrong – especially one of such exalted status."

"So I am guilty until I am proven to be innocent?" Mackenzie queried.

"No", answered the judge. "You are guilty until you are proven ready for sentencing – or public penance and repentance. Prosecutor – please commence your questioning of the Accused, in fact I should say, the Guilty. Sometimes even my political correctness needs correcting at times!"

"Citizen NP46", the Prosecutor began, "you are guilty of the sin of blasphemy. What have you to say for yourself?"

"Well, if denying global warming is blasphemy and you say that I have blasphemed then I must indeed be guilty of blasphemy. If you say so who am I to argue?" sneered Mackenzie.

The gallery let out a muffled titter.

"Silence", yelled the clerk to the gallery. This was clearly not a designated event for any display of humour.

"Why do you deny global warming?" asked the Prosecutor.

"Because the global warming period ended in 1998 and average global temperatures started dropping in 2005".

"And what authorities do you quote in making this ridiculous assertion".

"Nothing less than Hadley, NASA and the Goddard Institute for Space Studies".

"Yes, but an even greater authority contradicts all of these. The Politically Correct Bureau for Scientific Facts has said so".

"Well, I don't believe them".

"You are compounding your blasphemy boy, watch your tongue".

"Speaking of blasphemy compounding", intervened Benson, "there is another matter of which this youth is guilty. Please read it out most learned Politically Correct Prosecutor."

"It is this", hissed the Prosecutor through gritted teeth, "that this boy has actually denied that global warming is anthropogenic."

"Tell me EC NP46", said the judge, "if global warming is not man made, then how the deuce does it come about?"

"Fist of all, let me remind you that my name is not EC NP46. My name is Kenneth Mackenzie. For your information, weather cycles are related to sun spot activity, cosmic rays and the 10,000 year wobbles of the Earth on its orbit around the sun".

"Are you calling the great scientists in the Politically Correct Bureau for Scientific Facts liars? asked the Prosecutor.

"Oh no. Not at all. They are most definitely not that", answered Mackenzie sarcastically.

"Well I'm glad to hear that".

"They're just plain ignorant!"

"Enough, enough, stop, stop", yelled Benson. "I've had enough of your nonsense."

"And I've had enough of your stupidity", Mackenzie retorted.

The youth noticed that his mother had started sobbing. He felt sorry for her. He felt sorry for his father too. But his hot Scottish Celtic blood told him that he would be no slave to Political Correctness. His Christian conscience warned him to tell the truth. He simply could not control himself in the face of such provocation.

"Before I sentence you", said Benson who was now red in the face, "before I send you to the far north of Sweden to a rehabilitation camp for re-education and diversity training in the art of political correctness, you will go to Room 505 in this court building where the chief scientist of PCBSF will straighten you out on matters scientific."

In Room 505, Professor Donald Morrison beckoned Mackenzie to a chair.

"Now Kenneth", began Morrison. "You spoke such a load of rubbish in the court. Do you seriously, I mean *seriously*, believe all that guff you came away with?"

"Not unless your guff sounds more convincing".

"Oh! My! You *are* a stubborn one, young Kenneth", said Morrison in soft yet threatening tones.

"I may be a bit of an odd ball, but if you wish to convince me of your alternative scientific theories, you'll have to provide the evidence – that is according to the recognised scientific method".

Morrison put his head between his hands and started shaking it. "Oh Kenneth, I don't have to prove anything. No evidence is needed. It – eh, huh, it just is."

"I don't mean to sound awkward, but that just isn't quite good enough for me. If you can't provide the evidence then I am absolved from having to accept whatever it is you are going to say".

"First of all let me tell you Kenneth that the Earth is at the centre of the universe. It does not orbit the sun. The cosmic rays which you mentioned during the court session are all mythological. The sun, the moon, the planets and the stars all orbit around the Earth. And by the way, the Earth is not a globe, it is a totally flat piece of political correctness. And it is only around 6,000 years old. Don't you agree?"

"The moon does indeed orbit the Earth, but you are wrong about all the rest. Anyway, I'm still waiting for your evidence for all of this".

"All right Kenneth, all right. Here is the evidence. All the politically correct scientists have said so. And remember – those who are politically correct can never err – that is why they are known as the 'correct'. Now then Kenneth", continued Morrison in even softer and more threatening tones, "I'm sure that even you can't argue with such incontrovertible facts as these. I know you are about to say how much you so truly agree with me and that you are a completely reformed character. Let me hear it Kenneth, let me hear it from your very own lips."

What Mackenzie then said caused Morrison to completely lose his cool and to call the guards to bring the Most Undoubtedly Guilty back into the court room. Fifteen minutes later, Benson, looking more dour than ever, entered the court and cast his gaze upon the Guilty.

"I understand", began the judge, "that you, em, eh, - how can I put this? Mmmm eh you told Professor Morrison that he should perform the procreative act upon himself. Professor Morrison tells me that in spite of all the trouble he went to in explaining some scientific facts to you, you stubbornly refused to see reason. You are now guilty of the most serious and heinous sin of Sacrilege. What do you have to say for yourself now?"

"Nothing. But I have something to say to you."

"Lad, I hope that your words of sincere repentance are about to flow from your lips and into my ears".

Mackenzie merely stuck out his tongue and let out a long and loud rasping sound.

"That's the last straw", screamed Benson. "I hereby sentence you to three years of hard labour in the Kiruna Rehabilitation Camp in the north of Sweden for Politically Incorrect Recalcitrants."

At this point, the door of the court opened and in walked a strange looking figure. He was lank and lean and wore a long black gown that reached down to his feet. The entire court fell into a hushed silence as the strange man made his way to the dais. The judge and all the court officials immediately rose to their feet. Benson was the first to break the silence.

Wringing his hands and stroking his chin, he said "Oh the Most High and Mighty European Representative of Political Correctness for Mid-Region 12! We are most honoured by your most reverend and holy presence in this court".

The Representative made no response to Benson's outburst of obsequiousness. Wasting no time on formalities, he pointed a long bony finger at Mackenzie and asked, "Is this the irreverent, irreligious, blaspheming and sacrilegious individual?"

"Oh yy y eeess great Representative, it is", answered the cowering Benson.

"I am minded to come to this court today because of the seriousness of this case. I understand that the boy is willfully and stubbornly obstinate."

"Oh no doubt about that most great Representative. He most assuredly is".

"I don't give a damn who you are", Mackenzie blurted out. "I'm not succumbing to your political correctness."

"How dare you speak like that in front of such exulted holiness", cried Benson.

"Send him to the Kiruna Camp immediately", ordered the Representative. "And send him there until he recants his political incorrectness. The sentence is open. If he fails to recant and repent, he can stay there for the rest of his life."

"Your Most Exulted Reverence, may I suggest that this boy remain in the dock and hear some of the other politically incorrect cases? It may help him to see reason," Benson suggested.

"This court is highly merciful", said the Representative. "Let him stay and bring on the next Guilty".

Mackenzie returned to the dock. The next 'guilty' was a woman of about 35.

"Flora Fraser", boomed out Benson, "a complaint has been made against you that you have denied that the moon is made of green cheese".

"Who is the accuser?" inquired the Representative. "Bring him on."

A young man of about 20 entered the court.

"Who are you?" asked Benson.

"I am Angus Davidson and I have discovered that the moon is really and truly made of green cheese. And this woman has denied it."

"Well, I must admit that this is a new one on me", said Benson. "What a ridiculous and ludicrous assertion. You must be half mad boy. Are you a scientist?"

"No", was merely Davidson's reply.

"Then what qualifies you to make such an outrageous and silly claim? Are you wasting the court's time with schoolboy pranks."

"No", was again the boy's reply. I am not playing games and I am qualified."

"But you said you were not a scientist. How can you be so audacious as to make such a bold statement on the composition of the moon?"

The Youth took out a sheaf of papers and handed them to the clerk.

"Proceed to read them out", Benson ordered the clerk.

The clerk started reading: "1st class Honours in Political Correctness. MA in Advanced Politically Correct Studies. PhD in Politically Correct Multi-culturalism. Post doctoral research in Politically Correct Diversity."

Everyone in the court was struck dumb. The youth simply gawked around him grinning and smirking. The silence was broken by the Representative.

"This lad is obviously a genius. To have all these magnificent qualifications at so young an age means that he must have started learning about the solemnities of Political Correctness from childhood."

The youth by now was beaming. He was almost floating three feet off the ground.

"Then", said Benson somewhat gravely, "I hereby pronounce that the moon is indeed made of green cheese. Accept my apologies boy. How could I have been so blind? But it is only a genius like your good self who could possibly have come up with such an amazing scientific discovery. The future of the nation of Europe depends upon brilliant young minds like yours."

The Representative then put his oar in for the young man: "I hereby make it abundantly clear that anyone who is found guilty of being a denier of the green cheese composition of the moon will be pronounced a heretic and a blasphemer and sentenced to five years hard labour."

"Did the Apollo astronauts come back to Earth with loads of green cheese?" yelled Mackenzie. "To the best of my knowledge they found only rocks and dust".

Benson now turned to the Chief Scientist at the PCBSF. "Professor, would you like to make a comment on that silly statement?"

"Well, it's patently obvious now that the Apollo moon missions were faked", said Morrison.

"Why is that?" sneered Mackenzie.

"Because", said Morrison taking a deep breath to signify his impatience, "if they had been genuine, they would have brought back samples of green cheese. That they didn't, proves that the moon landings were a hoax."

"That all rests on the premise that the moon is actually made of green cheese", said Mackenzie grinning at the Chief Scientist.

"The underlying premise has been proven beyond all doubt. The great figures of Political Correctness have said so".

Angus Davidson intervened: "I have just had a great mental revelation. May I say something Your Political Correctness?"

"Go straight ahead young genius", answered Benson.

"If the Apollo missions had been real, then the lunar module would have sunk into the green cheese. A substance as soft as green cheese could never have taken the weight of the craft that was supposed to have landed on the moon's surface".

"A brilliant insight", added Morrison. "Now why didn't I think of that? Your Political Correctness, I want this lad brought onto the PCBSF team".

"He will be a great asset to the organisation", commented Benson.

Davidson started to gawk around the court with his juvenile grinning and beaming.

Benson now turned to Flora Fraser who now stood shaking and quivering in the witness stand. "Now my dear, what have you got to say for yourself."

"N n n now I I I understand", stammered Flora. How blind and utterly stupid I was".

Flora burst into a flood of uncontrollable sobbing.

"There, there now my dear", said Benson in affectionate tones. Even the most holy Representative here and I were unaware of this incontrovertible fact until now. But, like us, you have accepted the indisputable truth."

"Th th th thank you", sobbed Flora.

"Now dry your eyes my dear", said the Representative. "I've got a nice surprise here for you. Something which will cheer you up quite a bit."

The Representative took a rectangular card from his briefcase and put it on his desk. He signed it and gave it to the clerk of the court.

"Now give this to European citizen 698Bxxc", the Representative ordered the clerk.

The clerk walked over to the witness stand and handed the document over to Miss Fraser.

"Oooooh!" exclaimed an overjoyed Flora. "It's a Certificate of Political Correctness. Oh thank you Your Political Correctness for this Certificate of Political Correctness from the Politically Correct Court of Political Correctness. Oh thank you, thank you, thank you – everyone. Thank you again. Thank you a thousand times."

"You're very welcome", said the clerk. "Now, you run along like a good little girl and show that certificate to your mummy and daddy and all your friends".

The overjoyed Flora left the court in tears of ecstasy.

The next case involved three young lads who were charged as follows:

"Citizen 3345nsn3 is charged with telling a joke. Citizens jgh56jhn and 5jghn09 are charged with laughing at the joke", said the clerk reading from the charge sheet.

"Don't you know that it is a politically correct offence to display anything like a sense of humour?" said Benson with a most disapproving look on his face

"We are sorry, very sorry Your Political Correctness", muttered the boys.

"I should think so too. Laughing and guffawing is completely out of politically correct order".

"We understand. It won't happen again."

"And what exactly was the joke".

Citizen 3345nsn3 proceeded to relate the piece humour to the judge. "Why did the chicken cross the road?"

"And the answer to this ridiculous and silly question?"

"Because it wanted to get to the other side".

Benson and all the representatives of Political Correctness went red in the face.

"I am profoundly shocked at this breach of puritanical Political Correctness", Benson blurted out. "The court is adjourned for half an hour".

"What about sentencing these miscreants?" asked the clerk of the court whose face was now redder and whose hand was across his mouth.

"Nothing, nothing. Just, just eh, get them out of this court immediately, now, now, now," replied Benson who also had his hand across his mouth and whose face was of the same hue as the clerk's.

Only the European Representative for Political Correctness failed to go red in the face and cover his mouth with his hand.

"Why are you adjourning and why are you letting these hoodlums off so lightly?" the Representative asked Benson.

Benson, redder still and with his hand dropping slightly from his mouth replied, "this filthy, racist, fascist, Nazi joke makes us all so sick that we must take time to recover. You see how it so deeply offends our politically correct sensibilities".

Benson and the court officials left the chamber and hastened to their respective rooms. When they were inside their rooms and offices and thus out of sight of each other, they fell into the most phenomenal fits of hysterical laughter, the likes of which they had never before in their lives experienced. Their thoughts were essentially this: 'I've heard jokes before. Certainly this is not the first time I've heard wise cracks, but this one beats them all. This is the most hilarious joke I've ever heard'.

Half an hour later, Benson re-assembled the court. Only the European Representative for Political Correctness genuinely failed to understand the joke. Angus Davidson understood the joke but was so shocked that he fainted and had to be carried out on a stretcher and attended to by paramedics. Not to be outdone by Davidson (who had genuinely passed out) the Religious Enforcer of Politically Correct Doctrine (who did not understand the joke) feigned a faint. However he managed to tell the paramedics that his shock was worse than Davidson's and that he would need a respirator, so, hurry it up, and, later, what took you so long!

Benson had this to say: "Let all those in attendance today understand that the joke which those hooligans found so funny is an attack on the rights of animals. A chicken crossing the road could be run over. It could have been fleeing from a non-vegetarian. It may have been being led into a trap by a meat-eater. We must be more sensitive to bird psychology."

Benson then turned to Mackenzie: "I notice that you didn't laugh", he told the lad. "Do I take it you are now politically corrected?"

Mackenzie answered: "I was neither ignorant of the joke like that dunderhead of a religious enforcer nor did I have to pretend shock like he did nor feel genuine shock like Davidson. The joke is simply not funny. But I'm glad that you and the rest of the court found it to be so. Simple minds are easily pleased. Anyway, I hope you had a good laugh behind the scenes".

"Enough of your haughty impertinence", screamed Benson.

"How about this one, you politically correct dim-shit? There was a Jew, an Italian and a Saudi. They were waiting to be admitted by St. Peter into Heaven through the Pearly Gates. However, they were informed that there was to be a test before they could be admitted. The Italian was told that he had to be able to pass by any Italian restaurant and not be tempted to go in by the smell of the delicious cooking. The Jew was told that if he were to see any money lying on the ground, he should pass it by and leave it. For the Saudi – his test was simply that he must keep his hands off male backsides. Anyway, the three of them were walking in the street and they came near to an Italian restaurant. The wonderful aroma of the pasta and spaghetti was just too much for the Italian. He succumbed to the temptation and went in. So, he went to hell. The Jew and the Saudi were walking along the street. All of a sudden the Jew saw a coin lying on the ground. The sweat started to pour off him as he tried to resist. However, the temptation was too much for him. He bent down to pick up the coin – and they both went to hell".

There was a stunned silence in the court.

"Was that a joke?" Benson asked.

"Yes".

The clerk of the court went up to the bench and spent one minute whispering in Benson's ear.

"Has the clerk explained the joke to you well? Understand it now dumb ass?"

"I…I…. I understood it well enough. The..eh the clerk and I were discussing the eh kind of sentence you should be given. You have grossly insulted our Saudi allies. Don't you know Saudis are our allies".

"Your allies, Creep – not mine. And it doesn't surprise me that the Saudis are your allies. The irrationality of extremist Wahabi Islam dovetails well with the irrationality of Political Correctness."

"Silence! Enough!" yelled Benson

After a few more cases were heard before Mackenzie and the Representative, Kenneth Mackenzie was brought back to the witness box.

"Now laddie", commenced Benson. "Are you willing to see reason"?

"I've always seen it, it's you lot I'm worried about."

"I have tried every which way but loose to be kind to you. Yet, you remain as impertinent and insulting as ever."

"I ask you directly", intervened the Representative, "do you believe in global warming, the geo-centric model of the cosmos and the green cheese composition of the moon"?

Mackenzie took a deep breath, gritted his teeth and blurted out: "go and royally f**** yourself".

"That does it", screamed the Representative, "take him immediately to the labour camp in the north of Sweden. I sentence him to fifteen years of very hard labour. You not only blaspheme and utter sacrilegious statements but use foul and abusive language as well. You are not fit to live in politically correct society".

"There is something at least upon which we can both agree", answered Mackenzie.

"Get him in chains right now. No more delay."

At this, Mackenzie's mother started weeping. Her husband put a comforting arm around her. Suddenly a great commotion was heard in the corridors outside of the main court-room. The doors of the court-room burst open and in walked a figure in full medieval armour. Everyone, politically correct and politically incorrect were stunned into silence.

"What is this?" hollered Benson. "How dare you perform such stunts in the sacred precincts of a politically correct court. Guards! Guards! Arrest this idiot this very instant."

Five guards came rushing up to the man in armour, but the knight heavied them aside as though they were mere lightweight feathers.

"I'm sorry Your Political Correctness", said one of the guards as he picked himself up from the floor, "but this thing has knocked out every guard in the court house".

"In the name of the Most Holy President of the European Nation, I command you to halt and reveal yourself", the Representative commanded. But the armour clad knight just clanked his heavy step; and he made his way towards Kenneth Mackenzie.

The knight took Mackenzie by the arm and started to lead him out of the court house.

"Open fire on them, open fire on them right now", screamed the representative.

One of the guards aimed his gun at the knight. The bullet passed through him and so left him unharmed. It ricocheted off the desk in front of the dais.

"Fire on Mackenzie, fire on Mackenzie", screamed Benson.

Again, the guard fired on Mackenzie. And, miraculously, the bullet passed straight through him. Not only did it pass straight through him without causing the least harm to his body, but it struck the Representative in the stomach. The Representative immediately sank to his knees. A few seconds later he fell flat on his face dead.

"You are guilty of deicide, you are guilty of deicide Mackenzie", Benson shouted. "You have murdered a high figure of Political Correctness. You will be executed for this. Deicide, deicide, deicide!"

"I am not the one who fired the shot", protested Mackenzie.

"The bullet passed through you".

"I had nothing to do with that. I can't explain how it happened".

"It doesn't matter. I, I, I the great judge of politically correct matters have said you are guilty of deicide, so deicide you are guilty of", said Benson in a fit of hysteria.

The Politically Correct Religious Enforcer stood up and in reverend tones said: "Let us invoke the most holy trinity to dispel this politically incorrect evil".

The judge and all the court officials immediately extended their right hands in an upwards position thus initially giving a Nazi-style salute. They all began "in the name of Jean Monnet". Then lowering their hands downwards and slightly to the left, they continued the incantation with "and of Jacques Delors". Moving their hands over to the right they completed a pyramidal sign with the final incantation of the doxology "and of Jacques Santer". This was rounded off by intoning a passionate "EEEEEEE YOOOOO".

The mysterious knight in armour moved towards the court-house door with Mackenzie in his full and firm grip.

The guards opened fire again. People had to duck for cover as the bullets passed harmlessly through Mackenzie and his rescuer. In the corridor some guards both behind and in front of Mackenzie and the knight opened fire. The guards simply ended up killing each other!

The knight led Mackenzie to a horse. The knight sat on the horse and pulled Mackenzie up behind him. The two rode off together.

CHAPTER 3.
Junkies'Junk.

In a remote region of Columbia, Pedro Gonzagos, the biggest drug baron in Latin America, received a packet from his biggest client for the latest consignment of illegal narcotics.

"Please have a drink while we load your transport plane with the eh.... goods Herr Mulinger", said Gonzagos to his guest.

"Thank you", said Mulinger. "A whisky please".

Herr Mulinger was one of those ultra-efficient types and a man of few words. He said what was necessary and no more. By contrast, Gonzagos was a talkative Latino, but he soon learned not to ask questions. Why Mulinger and his organisation were interested in purchasing such vast quantities of heroine and cocaine was something which Gonzagos very soon learned not to inquire into. However powerful Pedro Gonzagos might be, Herr Friedrich Mulinger was infinitely more so. Although never actually put into so many words, Gonzagos knew it was simply a case of 'take the money and keep your mouth shut'. And Mulinger gave Gonzages his 'packets' which seldom contained less than one million dollars at a time.

Who Mulinger was and who his 'colleagues' were, were no-go areas in the short conversations between Mulinger and Gonzagos.

The routine was exactly the same. Gonzagos received a coded email from Mulinger that he would be paying a visit in a month for x amount of x drug or drugs. A month later, Mulinger's plane would touch down on the private piece of air-strip just outside Gonzagos' poppy plantation. Gonzagos would be waiting for him in person. He would then drive his most valuable customer to his bungalow in the middle of his estate. On average it took half an hour to load up Mulinger's transport plane with the contraband. While the loading was getting underway, Mulinger would have his whisky and his 'conversation' with Gonzagos. Then, one of Gonzagos' minions would enter to announce that the plane was loaded and ready for take-off. At this point, Mulinger would down the remains of his whisky and in brusque military style, march smartly out of the bungalow in almost goose-step fashion. This visit was no different from the innumerable visits Mulinger had paid Gonzagos over the last 30 years or so. In fact it was no different to the visits which Mulinger's father, grandfather, great grandfather and great great grandfather had made to Gonzagos' father, grandfather, great grandfather and great great grandfather over the many decades since the end of the Second World War way back in 1945, almost 80 years previously. Gonzagos drove his most valued client to the air-strip. As he watched Friedrich Mulinger's plane take off, he witnessed the same old routine that his father, grandfather, great grandfather and great great grandfather before him had witnessed but never could explain: as the plane ascended to around 15,000 feet, a disk-shaped saucer mysteriously descended from a much higher elevation and took Mulinger and his grizzly wares on board. The 'UFO' moved off and the transport plane exploded in mid-air.

CHAPTER 4.
Inside The Cave.

Kenneth Mackenzie and his strange knight rescuer galloped for many miles. During their two hour journey on horseback, Mackenzie had tried to ask the knight questions as to who he was and why the two had managed to defy death in such a charmed manner. The knight, however, made no reply. He remained silent throughout their horseback journey.

At last Mackenzie and the knight came to a cave. It was a cave which Mackenzie recognised. It was the cave where the great Scottish king, Robert the Bruce, while hiding from his English enemies had seen a spider attempting to climb to up its web. The spider had to make many attempts to reach the top. The spider kept slipping back, but it never gave up: finally it did succeed in getting to where it wanted to be. This observation of the spider gave Bruce heart in his fight against the English; it made him coin the adage with which we are all familiar with today – 'if at first you don't succeed, try, try, try again'. The significance of the cave and why the knight had brought him there was beginning to dawn on young Kenneth. Rescuer and rescued descended from the horse. At last the knight spoke: "I am Black Douglas. We have a mission to rescue Scotland from the tyrannies of political correctness. First of all, Scotland, and then the rest of the British Isles."

It was now Mackenzie's turn to be speechless. "I… I don't quite…. I mean how, who, … I…."

"Kenneth, you have been through a lot. Your mind is in turmoil. You have so many questions you want to ask. But fear not, brave one, all will be revealed to you in due course. Be patient".

The knight then proceeded to take off his helmet.

"You really are Black Douglas", exclaimed Mackenzie. "You are just as the paintings portray you".

"Go into King Robert's cave Kenneth – and you will learn much".

"But the cave has been closed for a long time. It has been sealed with a massive steel door. It has been closed for years now".

When the United States of Europe became the unitary state called simply 'Europe' in 2015, places of historical interest and shrines of national heritage were off-limits as they were considered as being 'politically incorrect'. The only relevant history was the history of the processes which led up to the final elimination of the nation states of true Europe of which 'Europe' was the culminating point.

Black Douglas pointed towards the cave. Mackenzie watched as the door slowly but surely began to open. In three minutes, a gaping entrance revealed itself to Mackenzie. It was something he thought he would never see in his life. King Robert the Bruce's cave was now open! The boy wheeled round with the intention of asking Black Douglas' permission to enter, but the Douglas was gone. Mackenzie looked around but Black Douglas was nowhere to be seen. Slowly and cautiously, Mackenzie made his way towards the mouth of the cave.

Young Kenneth was not quite sure what to expect inside the cave. He had been taken to Bruce's cave by his parents when he was just a toddler so he had only the vaguest of recollections about the cave's interior. For fifteen minutes he sat in the cave but nothing happened. "Is all this some sort of joke?" he asked himself "Perhaps I was a fool to believe this guy who called himself 'Black Douglas'. Yet, the bullets passed straight through him – and me. So this does look like some sort of visitation from another dimension. Oh, am I only dreaming this?"

Another fifteen minutes elapsed – nothing. Mackenzie started walking around the cave. "Hello", he shouted at the top of his voice. "Hello, hello – can anyone hear me? Is there anyone there? What am I supposed to do?" It was like the prophets of Baal invoking their god when in contest with Elias. Nothing happened! After spending a full forty minutes in the cave, Mackenzie felt that he had been patient long enough and so decided to leave. He turned round in the direction of the cave's opening and to his horror found that it had been blocked. And not only had it been blocked but it simply wasn't there. The entire cave took on a completely new dimension. Instead of a small pokey little cave, a massive cavern was presented to Kenneth Mackenzie. Torches of fire lit up the cavern. Mackenzie decided to start exploring. The part of the cave he was in did not reveal anything to him, apart from its immense size and burning torches. He walked the entire length of the 'room' until he came to a narrow passage way of about five feet in width and ten feet in length. This led the boy into another room even more massive than the previous one. The first thing he noticed were shields, flags, tapestries and escutcheons hanging from the cave roof and from its walls and all bearing the imprints of ancient Scottish heraldry. Mackenzie stopped for about ten minutes to look at these magnificent works of art. He then proceeded further and further into the gigantic room. Half- way along the room, he beheld a most astonishing sight; the heraldic drapes gave way to a scene of hundreds of suits of medieval armour all laid out on slabs. He walked along slowly gazing with an awe-struck gaze at the knightly regalia. One particular suit of armour particularly caught his attention. He recognised it. He had seen it only a few hours earlier. With fear and trembling, the lad walked over to it. With shaking and unsteady hands he started to slowly lift the visor up. By now Mackenzie was breathing heavily with fear. When he had at last mustered the courage to lift the visor completely up, he saw the face of Black Douglas.

Mackenzie doubled up in a horrendous fit of choking and sweating. He could barely find his voice.

"Bl… Black Doug.. Doug Douglas. Wh Wh Where am I?", the boy stammered.

But Black Douglas remained stiff and lifeless in his suit of armour. Gingerly, Mackenzie placed his hand on Black Douglas' forehead. The knight was cold to the touch, his body rigid with the inflexibility of a cadaver. Mackenzie replaced the helmet. It was clear to him now that he had entered a burial place for the knights of the ancient Kingdom of Scotland. He walked on. It was a full five minutes before the end of the room was in sight. At the far end of the room, Kenneth descried a raised platform. On the platform was a throne-like seat. And on the throne sat one in kingly raiment. Kenneth stopped in his tracks.

"Approach me", said the king in a commanding tone.

Kenneth obeyed the royal summons.

"Kneel down lad", the king ordered the boy.

Kenneth knelt down.

As if he could read the boy's mind, the king informed Mackenzie, "I am indeed, King Robert the Bruce of Scotland".

The Bruce held a massive unsheathed sword in an upright position in his right hand. He arose from the throne maintaining the sword upright and walked down the three steps of the dais towards Mackenzie. He brought the sword down towards the boy and touched each of his shoulders with its point. In a booming voice, the king roared out, "Arise Sir Kenneth Mackenzie".

"Thank you, thank you Your Majesty", said Sir Kenneth. "But I am young and I fear that I have not really done anything of worthwhile note to deserve this great honour".

"You haven't Kenneth, you haven't", replied the king, "but you will Sir Kenneth, you will".

The king sheathed his sword and at once became more relaxed and informal. He bade the young knight to enter another room. This one was more massive than the previous one.

"What an amazing place", thought Mackenzie. "Each section of this cave is more massive than the one before". The cave was dimly lit and it was difficult for Kenneth to make out very much. However, very slowly the cave started to brighten up. It appeared that someone was lighting wall torches. In five minutes, the cave was fully lit up.

The light revealed to Kenneth a huge table laden with the choicest of food and drink.

"I'm sure that after your ordeal at that kangaroo court, you could eat a hearty meal", said King Robert to his guest.

"Yes, Your Majesty. I very much could", replied Robert.

The King took his place at the head of the table and invited Kenneth to sit at his right hand. There was then the sound of a trumpet blast and hundreds of prelates, lords, ladies, knights, squires and esquires trooped into the great hall and took their places at the magnificent table. The fare was magnificent. All partook of boar, venison, duck and fish with the choicest of wines to accompany. The meal was eaten in total silence. An hour later, the meal was finished and the King stood up. The nobility of Scotland arose and walked out of the hall in magnificent procession. The King and Kenneth returned to the throne room.

"We ate the meal in sad silence Kenneth because all of Scotland, past and present, are in a most terrible grief at what has happened to this great land", explained the King.

The King and Kenneth were joined by Black Douglas and four other personages. They were introduced to Kenneth by Black Douglas as William Wallace, Rob Roy MacGregor, Robert Burns and Sir Walter Scot.

"William Wallace, Rob Roy and I fought for the honour of Scotland", said the Douglas. "And Robert Burns and Sir Walter Scott wrote for the honour of Scotland".

"You must fight for your native land Sir Kenneth", said Rob Roy to the boy.

"You have a great task before you", said Wallace.

"One day you will compose great poetic works on your mighty deeds', Burns advised him.

"And your narrations on how Scotland was freed from its present tyranny will astonish the world", Scott informed the boy.

"I am one man only", protested Kenneth. "What exactly is my task? How can I accomplish it single handedly?"

"You will be guided Kenneth", said Wallace.

"All will unfold all in good time", added Rob Roy.

Suddenly there was what appeared to be a great rumble of thunder and a bolt of light. The throne room became lit with an unearthly glow. A figure appeared about 20 feet away from the group. It was that of a man. He was covered in blood and full of wounds, yet on his head he wore a crown. The bloodied figure directed his gaze towards Kenneth.

"William Shakespeare wrote of me", said the ghastly spectre. "I am King Duncan of Scotland. The traitor Macbeth tried to usurp my throne and my kingly right. Sadly, the nation of Scotland has given birth to many Macbeths. What you see now Kenneth is exactly how I was when Macbeth's dagger made its murderous plunges into my body. What you now observe boy, is symbolic of what has happened to Scotland. The manner of my death was a pre-figuration of the brutal murder of an entire nation. The dagger is the dagger of political correctness".

With that – the bloody shade of King Duncan disappeared.

"You must leave this cave and make your way to Canada", said King Robert.

"What shall I do there, Sire?"

"Study at the University in Nova Scotia. It teaches real science".

"Sire. My main concern is this: my parents. I cannot leave them. In fact I now fear for their welfare if not for their very lives. I am now a fugitive. While I am in this cave, while I am completely in another space/time dimension, I am safe. Soon, however, I must return to the harsh realities of the 21st century. The police will be scouring the countryside for me. I am certain they will arrest my mum and dad. I cannot do anything until I can be certain of their safety."

King Robert the Bruce looked compassionately at the young lad and assured him that he need not worry about his parents.

"Kenneth. Your parents are no longer in this world".

Mackenzie shrunk back in horror.

"You mean they are dead!"

"No".

"I don't understand. What do you mean 'they are not in this world'?"

"I mean simply just that, Sir Kenneth".

"Will I ever see them again? I....I.... I... mean in this world."

"Both in this world and in another – but first in another."

"Can you please, Your Majesty, tell me plainly where they are?"

"That will be revealed to you when the time is right. Until then Kenneth, Sir Kenneth, show knightly strength and patience".

At this Kenneth asked no more questions regarding the whereabouts of his parents but instead trusted in the monarch's kingly word.

CHAPTER 5.

A Vile Blast From The Nasty Past.

"You look rather puzzled about something, Sir Kenneth", commented the King to his guest.

"It is something which has perplexed me for a long time", answered the young knight.

"What is it?" asked King Robert.

"Why has political correctness taken such a hold in most of the Western World? Why only in the West? Why is it that the more ludicrous it becomes, the more that people seem to acquiesce in it? Why is it that only a few people see it for the utter balderdash that it most undoubtedly is? I simply can't fathom it out".

"Kenneth, you are about to find out exactly why. You are about to see something that will shake you to the core. After you have seen what you are about to see, you will, politically incorrect as you are, find yourself having to revise, nay, revolutionise, your entire political cosmology".

With that a white cloud enveloped King Robert and he disappeared from sight. In his place stood a mighty archangel.

"I am St. Michael the Archangel, Prince and Commander of the Heavenly Host", the angelic visitor told the young knight.

Mackenzie was awestruck. The archangel looked fearsome. Yet there was nothing frightening about him. Mackenzie's parents had always told him that those who strive to lead a good and honest life need fear nothing from heavenly visitors.

"You wish to know why the pernicious doctrine of political correctness has taken such a strong hold in these islands?" continued St. Michael.

"Yes…y..yy…yes I do", stammered the lad.

The archangel pointed towards the far end of the cave room. A swirling vortex seemed to open up. After around two minutes, there stood within the vortex, a figure of whose identity there could be no mistaking. Kenneth Mackenzie shrunk back in horror at the shade of Adolph Hitler.

"He, better than anyone else, can answer your questions", said the archangel.

"I will say nothing", snarled the shade of the Fuhrer.

St. Michael then became brighter and more radiant; in a most powerful and commanding voice, he called out to the most evil person who had ever lived, "in the name of the Most High God you will speak as I command you to".

The Fuhrer shrunk back in fear and trembling when so strongly confronted by the mighty archangel.

"All right, all right. You see Mackenzie, I escaped from the bunker in 1945. In fact hundreds escaped with me through a labyrinth of underground railway networks. Scientists, engineers, politicians, financiers, medical doctors and many more all escaped the clutches of the allies."

"And what was the purpose in all of this?" Kenneth wanted to know.

"It was to continue the war in a very different and subtle way", answered Hitler. "You thought you had won the war. Wrong! You simply had won the military conflict. The war went on and I can assure you of this *we are winning it.* We have been winning it since 1945."

"I don't quite understand how", said Kenneth. "Elaborate on it".

"I refuse to say any more", answered Hitler.

At this, St. Michael the Archangel glowed brighter than ever. Hitler, becoming more afraid than ever, continued his discourse.

"Well Mackenzie, we have been using a number of tactics to undermine the allies. First of all we set up the Common Market, which became the EU, which in turn became the United States of Europe and which is now the unitary state of Europe. This was our blueprint for Europe which we would have put into effect had we beaten the allies militarily. Our Nazi agenda was for a Europe of regions and not a Europe of nation states."

"And your other tactics? Tell me about those you piece of sick nastiness", demanded Mackenzie.

"It was to flood Europe with third world immigrants so as to undermine the social, political and cultural cohesiveness of the nation states".

Once more, Hitler relapsed into silence.

Once again St. Michael glowed. This time his glow became even brighter. He yelled at the Fuhrer with a booming voice – the kind that surely only an archangel could possess.

"Tell Sir Kenneth about Political Correctness", the archangel commanded.

The shade of the Fuhrer shook with fear as he began to expound on Political Correctness.

"Our master stroke was to invent the pseudo philosophy of Political Correctness. Initially, the underlying basis of this philosophical system was to brand those who opposed immigration as 'fascist' and 'Nazi'. Those who objected to the European integrationist processes were to be considered as 'extremist' and 'narrow-minded nationalists' – those who stood in the way of peace and progress. In fact, another great master stroke was to equate nationalism with Nazism. In fact, international socialism has nothing to do with genuine nationalism. Few there were, and are, who are bright enough to see this. Those who railed against the absence of the mention of God in the European constitution were branded as 'bigots' and 'fascists' or 'religious fanatics and zealots'. Yet no-one hurt the Christian churches in Germany and beyond more than we did. The Politically Correct think they are being so liberal and democratic when they embrace the philosophy of Deep Ecology and Earth Worship. So we have convinced many, even the so-called 'right wingers', of the illusion of global warming. Little do they know that occultism and paganism are the very religious and philosophical underpinnings of Nazism. And then we have birth control and euthanasia. Oh how those who advocate it think they are being so 'left wing'. In fact, we practiced it with a passion in Nazi Germany. The sick, elderly and feeble minded were eliminated. We practiced infanticide where we found babies who had been born with physical or mental defects. All this has been achieved. As the decades rolled on, Political Porrectness became more and more refined. In fact, it became refined to the point of lunacy and idiocy – no Christmas trees and church bells incase Muslims were offended – you know what I'm talking about Mackenzie, you saw examples of it in court today. We also pulled off a great one with regard to 'multiculturalism' and 'diversity'. Those who oppose these doctrines are in fact the genuine multiculturalists and diversifiers. Our plan is to undermine national cultures with immigration. Under the name of 'multiculturalism', we can in fact create a global syncretistic monoculture. This greatly smoothes our path towards the One World Government to which we aspire. You see, genuine multiculturalism and diversity can only exist if every nation maintains its own peculiar culture. So you see, the useful idiots in the politically correct movement, are greatly facilitating the Nazi plan. They are inadvertently helping to set up the Fourth Reich."

"And what about your future plans? When would you consider the Second World War as being officially over?" Mackenzie asked Hitler.

"When we achieve One World Government".

"And how do you plan to do that?"

"Other regional blocs, similar to Europe, are nearing completion. There is one that embraces the Americas called the Organisation of American States. Then there is the Association of South East Asian States. Then, we have the Organisation of African Unity. Also there is Eastern Europe and Eurasia which takes in the former Soviet satellite countries, Russia and the former Soviet Republics and Japan. The Middle Eastern nations will unite under OPEC. All these will merge to become The Government of Earth."

"Is this the New World Order that George Bush senior spoke of?"

"Precisely", snarled the Fuhrer.

"What exactly is your connection with the Saudis?"

"They approve of what we did to the Jews. They cheer my gas chambers. They greatly applaud my extermination camps."

"Now. Here is the most mystifying thing for me. How come people like myself are termed 'Nazis' and 'fascists' because we are politically incorrect?"

"That is part of the deceptive strategy we have been pursuing. The vast majority of those in the ranks of Political Correctness are, what we might say, 'useful idiots'. Only a small number of elite know the reality. The vast majority of the Politically Correct think they are being 'anti-Nazi'. Little do they know it but they are helping the Nazi cause."

"This is an evil and wicked tactic. You are playing upon people's gullibility".

"Oh, it's an old, old tactic", sniggered the Fuhrer. The Knights Templar were charged with the task of defending orthodoxy. And where do you think heresy finds its safest shelter? Of course, within the constructs of where you would least expect to find it?" said the Fuhrer answering his own question. "Where is the safest place for a fly which wants to escape being sprayed? On the spray can itself".

"One last question before you go back to where you belong: how have only a few hundred Nazis managed to penetrate the highest echelons of government, fooling the best and brightest in the world and perverting entire establishments? Explain that to me!"

"We were only a few hundred who escaped from the bunker and its environs. But now, there are thousands of us - we who are the real Nazis".

"Even so, how do you pervert millions? How do you make people so stupid?"

The shade of the Fuhrer started to fade. In less than half a minute, he was gone.

"Kenneth", said St. Michael. "That is a question which will be answered later in your life. For the moment, you must be patient."

CHAPTER 6.
Student Life.

The scene was now completely transformed. Kenneth now stood outside of the cave. Once more he was with The Douglas.

"What now?" asked the boy. "What is my future? Where do I take it from here? How do I pick up the pieces?"

"You are a fugitive Kenneth", answered Black Douglas. "You must be extremely careful about every move you make. However, you will be protected. You will go to King's College University in Halifax, Nova Scotia, Canada. There you will be enrolled in the Faculty of Science. It has all been arranged for you. A bank account has been opened for you with the Bank of Halifax. There is sufficient money there to take care of all your tuition and living expenses for the next four years. In the meantime, take this packet. It contains hard cash – enough to get you to Aberdeen where you can take a fishing boat to Norway. Take a flight from Oslo to Canada".

"I thank you for all of this great kindness. I am extremely grateful to you, King Robert and all whom I met in the cave. But, what happens to me after I graduate? What should I do? When will I see my parents again?"

"Do not worry Kenneth. All will be revealed to you. One step at a time my boy".

Kenneth Mackenzie found Halifax to be a big bustling city of around 150,000 people. The climate was the only thing that Kenneth found similar to his native Scotland. Kenneth lived in a small second floor flat of a large house located near King's College University. He seriously wondered if what had happened in the last week had all been a dream, a dream conjured up by the traumatic experiences of the court room vaudeville in his native Scotland. Yet, here he was in Canada, and at university. The bank account and the money were real – just as the Black Douglas had informed him.

As the months rolled on, Kenneth found university life to be exhilarating. He excelled in all his subjects. He made many friends but he did not relate his strange experiences to them. He had been cautioned by Black Douglas to tell no-one. Apart from anything else, he was afraid that his fellow students would think him to be mad. So Kenneth kept out of politics and well into his studies.

Although the lad devoted himself heart and soul to learning, the absence of politically correct nonsense greatly pleased him. He found the common sense both on campus and in town to be welcomingly refreshing from the idiocy he had encountered in what once had been Scotland. The scientists who tutored him were *real* scientists. There was none of the nonsense about a 6,000 year old Earth at the centre of the Universe, or about the moon being made of green cheese. In lighter moments, away from studying, he could share a joke or two with his friends, have a good laugh – and not be arraigned in a court for it.

It was only to his very close friend Hilary Jennings that Kenneth talked politics. Hillary was a lovely 18 year old blonde who lived in Halifax and who was of Scottish descent. Like Kenneth, she was a student at King's but was studying the Arts and Humanities.

"Of course, Political Correctness is at its most wild in Europe, but, you know Ken, Canada is not exactly the most politically incorrect country", explained Hilary to her boyfriend.

"But it's not exactly the most politically correct either", commented Kenneth.

"Oh, we have our share of politically correct nutters around the campus here, but they're kept in their place; they don't dominate as they do in Europe".

"You know Hilary, I'm a democrat. The PC types are entitled to their opinions; they are just simply not entitled to ram it down others' throats."

"That's the reasonable way of looking at things Ken".

"Where I come from – reason no longer exists."

The first term flew by and Kenneth Mackenzie came top of his class in Physics, Mathematics, Chemistry and Biology.

"I'm so pleased that you chose to study here Kenneth", said Professor James Carpenter, the Head of the Department of Physics.

"It's a great pleasure to be here", said Kenneth.

"We'll teach you real science here, my boy", the professor assured his young student.

It seemed to Kenneth that Carpenter was well aware of the appalling conditions to which academe hand sunk back in former Scotland.

"Kenneth", continued Carpenter, "the Chancellor of the University would like to see you at 2 o'clock this afternoon."

"The Chancellor!" exclaimed Kenneth. "Why does he want to see me?"

"I really have no idea Kenneth".

The Chancellor's secretary led the young student into a large palatial office.

"Ah! Come in Kenneth. It is so good to see you".

"You wanted to speak to me about something Chancellor".

"Oh I just wanted to see how you were faring at university. You must find it quite different to the educational system in Europe".

"Completely different Chancellor. My real education came from my parents. Schools now in Europe are merely indoctrination centres where pupils are drilled in politically correct doctrine".

"Here at King's College, we pride ourselves in free thinking. We as much encourage our students to give their ideas as we encourage them to absorb what they hear in lectures and tutorial sessions."

"It is this openness which I like so much about this University".

"Kenneth, graduation is still quite a few years away. However, I hope that you will become a member of Faculty when your studies are completed".

"Thank you Chancellor. I deeply appreciate the offer".

"Of course, I'm not asking you to make a lifetime's commitment to King's College University, just the few years of your doctoral studies".

"You mean, you're offering me the chance of doing a PhD? Whether or not I have the ability to do that very much depends upon the level of degree I eventually attain. If I may say so Chancellor – isn't it a bit premature to be considering doctoral studies?"

"You are far too humble Kenneth. If you are incapable of doctoral studies, then very few people are capable of it."

"Well, thank you sir".

"Think about it Kenneth. It is still quite a few years away yet, but, bear in mind what I have said."

"Wow!" exclaimed Hilary Jennings as she entered Kenneth's flat on December 25th to help Kenneth with the preparations for the Christmas dinner. "You've really gone to town on the Christmas tree and decorations. Oooo and a real Christmas tree too. Most people these days just go for artificial ones."

"Well, you know, the lands under the occupation of Europe are forbidden to celebrate Christmas. It's considered as being an extreme form of political incorrectness. It's supposed to be highly provocative and may offend Muslims and various other non-Christian sects".

"Ken", said Hilary thoughtfully. "Why don't you go back home at Christmastime. I know it isn't much fun now in your native Scotland, but… I mean, if I may say so…. Don't you want to see your parents and your family?"

The tears started to well up in Kenneth's eyes. When Hilary noticed the change in her boyfriend's countenance and general demeanour, she put a comforting arm around his shoulders and continued, "I'm so sorry Ken, are your parents..... are they... I mean.."

"They're OK", replied Ken. "But..... I can't return to Scotland".

"Why not dear?"

"Well, to cut a long story short, I'm persona non grata in my homeland because of my political incorrectness".

"I understand", replied Hilary. She instinctively knew not to ask any more questions on the matter.

"Anyway", said Kenneth brightening up a bit, "our first guests will be here soon, so we'd better get a move on with the food, hadn't we?"

CHAPTER 7.
Bizarre Events.

The years rolled by and Kenneth graduated with First Class Honours in Mathematics and Physics. He soon embarked upon his doctoral studies. He decided to do his thesis on the behaviour of sub-atomic particles in high temperatures. His supervisor was Dr. Terrence Artcliff. Hilary had graduated the same year and started her PhD studies in 15th century French poetry.

One morning, Kenneth went to see Professor Carpenter in the Faculty of Science building. He knocked on Carpenter's door, but there was no answer. He knocked a second time – still no response from within.

"This is strange" thought Kenneth to himself. Carpenter is always so punctual.

The floor of the Department of Physics where Carpenter's office was located was deserted, so there was no-one to whom Kenneth could enquire about Carpenter. After walking up and down the corridor somewhat aimlessly, he espied Carpenter's secretary just emerging at the top of the stairway; Kenneth hurried towards her.

"Have you seen Professor Carpenter?" Kenneth asked the secretary.

"Isn't he in his office?"

"Well, I knocked on his door but I got no reply".

"Perhaps he intends to come in a little bit later today."

"But I had an appointment to see him this morning".

"Mmmm – that's strange then that he's not here."

The secretary took out her mobile phone. "Let me phone his home", she said.

After a few seconds of conversation on the phone, the secretary informed Kenneth that the professor had left home that morning.

"You know", she said, "Professor Carpenter has been getting a little deaf these days. Perhaps he hasn't put his hearing aid in."

The secretary went over to the door and gave a very loud knock. Even this did not elicit any response. She tried his mobile number but with no luck. The office intercom likewise proved to be futile. She went over to the door and slowly turned the handle saying "Professor Carpenter, hello, are you there". She gingerly pushed open the door. When it was open far enough, she slowly poked her head in. It was at this point that she let out one almighty scream. Kenneth rushed forward to see what the mater was. There, lying on the carpet in front of his desk was Professor James Carpenter dead.

"How long had you known the deceased?" asked Tony Kent, the Halifax police chief.

"For almost five years", Kenneth replied

"Would you have any idea as to why someone would want to strangle Professor Carpenter?" continued the chief.

"None whatsoever. He was extremely well liked by his students. I never knew of him having any enemies."

"Do you know of anyone who would have benefited from Prof. Carpenter's death?"

"I have no idea. My relationship with the professor was purely student/teacher. I have no knowledge of his personal life."

"Now Mr. Mackenzie, I want to ask you something about your political views, if you don't mind".

"I do very much mind. This is my personal business and Canada is still a free country. Furthermore, I have never been involved in politics in this country, and, more so still, I fail to see what this could possibly have to do with Prof. Carpenter's death".

"It could well do so sir".

"I fail to see how. To the best of my knowledge, Prof. Carpenter was not involved in politics. In fact I don't even know what his political views were".

"Then you are not very well informed, Mr. Mackenzie. Prof. Carpenter quite often spoke out against politically correct philosophical concepts."

"Why should anyone want to kill him simply for that?"

The police chief looked at Kenneth in a very curious way. "You know Mr. Mackenzie", he eventually said, "I'm surprised to hear you say that. You, more than most people, know about the excesses of Political Correctness".

"I've known Political Correctness as being mere tomfoolery at best and stark raving insanity at worst. Yet, even where I come from, they don't murder people for their politically incorrect ideas, they send them off to remote gulags and re-education camps."

The police chief looked at Kenneth thoughtfully.

"Mr. Mackenzie, things have been changing very rapidly since you came to Canada. Political Correctness both here and in other parts of the world has been on the increase. People who have been known for their politically incorrect ideas have started changing their minds about many things. They are now seeing the world through PC tinted glasses. Perhaps you have been too engrossed in your studies to have noticed it."

"Chief Kent, I know that politically correct madness has been increasing throughout the world. I have not been totally cocooned in academe. In fact, this evil doctrine has been on the increase since as far back as the end of the Second World War in 1945."

"But it is only in the last couple of years that it has really taken off like never before."

"What I can't understand Chief, is that it all seems to be a one-way-street. We never hear of anyone abnegating their PC doctrines and embracing non-PC ways of thinking."

"We also find this perplexing, Mr. Mackenzie, very perplexing indeed".

The months rolled by and Kenneth, after coming to terms with the sad and tragic loss of his mentor and friend got back into the grind of his doctoral research.

"You've never really been the same since Prof. Carpenter's murder", Hilary told Kenneth as they were sitting drinking wine in Kenneth's flat.

"Well, it has come as a terrible blow. Professor Carpenter was an innocent and harmless man".

"He did speak out against PC ideas".

"Is that a reason to strangle someone to death?!"

"PCism doesn't get any less nasty Ken – if anything it gets worse all the time".

"You're right".

"Have the police got any clues as to who the culprit or culprits may be?"

"If they do, they certainly didn't tell me. But I feel they are clueless; at least that's the impression I got during my interview with Kent".

The following day, while Kenneth was working in his office, his 'phone rang.

"Kenneth Mackenzie speaking".

"Oh, good morning Kenneth".

"Good morning Miss Slater". It was the late Professor Carpenter's secretary – now secretary to his replacement Professor Terrence Artcliff.

"Are you busy right now?"

"Not really. Is there anything I can do for you?"

"The Chancellor would like to see you in his office immediately, if that is all right with you?"

"Sure. I'll go over right away."

Kenneth put on his jacket. It was winter and the cold bit hard. On his way over to the palatial structure which housed the Chancellor's apartments, Kenneth pondered on why the university's top man wanted to see him – and to see him in such a haste. When he entered the building, he was greeted by a very pleasant looking young lady.

"Mr. Mackenzie?"

"Yes".

"Please go straight up to the Chancellor's office. Go right in – he's expecting you".

Kenneth made his way up the long carpeted flight of stairs. The Chancellor's door was slightly ajar. Kenneth tapped lightly and walked in. What he saw inside almost gave him heart failure. The Chancellor was lying dead on the floor – strangled!

Kenneth dashed out of the room and downstairs.

"Hello Miss, Miss, where are you?!" he yelled. But the secretary had disappeared.

Kenneth dashed across the campus to the Department of Physics. He ran into Miss Slater's office and found her strangled to death. Kenneth was now at his wits end. As it was examination time, most of the students were in the exam halls and most of the staff were involved in invigilation. Kenneth tried to find someone. He stormed into his supervisor's room. Artcliff looked up in surprise at Mackenzie who was now sweating profusely.

"Good God – man!" exclaimed Artcliff. "What on Earth is going on?"

"The Chancellor has been murdered – Miss Slater has been murdered – come quickly".

"What are you talking about. Miss Slater is in her room. I spoke to her only five minutes ago."

Artcliff was horrified by what he saw when his pupil took him to the secretary's office.

"I'll call the police immediately", he said. Artcliff got on the line to police HQ in Halifax and explained the situation. Three minutes later he hung up and told Kenneth that they'd be at the university in about ten minutes. A few seconds later the 'phone rang. Artcliff listened and simple said, "yes, yes, of course. Sure".

Turning to Mackenzie, Artcliff said, "that was the police. They want you to wait outside the building for them and for me to stay with the body to ensure that nothing is disturbed".

Kenneth quickly made his way downstairs. The police turned up and scrambled out of their vehicle. Over by the Chancellor's building, Kenneth could see another police car.

"I'm Kenneth Mackenzie. I am the one who discovered the murders", he said to the policemen.

"Where is Terrence Artcliff?" asked a sergeant.

"He's upstairs with the body – just where you told him to be a few minutes ago".

The police officers gave each other puzzled looks.

Kenneth and the police officers dashed upstairs to find Artcliff lying next to his secretary and strangled to death!

"We can't help but notice Mr. Mackenzie that it has always been you who have found the bodies", said Chief Kent during a long interrogation at Halifax Police HQ.

"Not quite. It was Miss Slater who discovered Professor Carpenter's body".

"But you *were* at the scene of the murder".

"Chief Kent, are you considering me as a suspect?"

"No! The evidence does not point towards you. First of all, there are no finger prints and there is no organic material left behind from which our forensic squad could extract DNA. Secondly, we think you'd be intelligent enough to keep yourself away from the scenes of the crimes had you been the culprit."

"Well yes", Kenneth sighed.

"However, there are a couple of anomalies that need to be cleared up. You told the four policemen who arrived at the Department of Physics that Professor Artcliff had got a 'phone call from us advising you to wait downstairs to meet us and for the professor to wait by the corpse so as to guard against any disturbance of the evidence. No such 'phone call came from this office."

Kenneth gawked at the police chief in total bewilderment. Eventually he found his voice. "Then it must have been a trick by the murderer – or murderers – to get me out of the way in order to murder Artcliff."

"And possibly to frame you", the chief added.

"This means that the killer was hiding in the building and made a hasty exit from another part of the building".

"Obviously so. Now there is another reason we do not suspect you. Although you are young and strong, you are not quite strong enough to strangle a man of Artcliff's fairly large frame in a few minutes. In all of the cases there were no signs of struggle. Every object in each murder scene was in place. Frankly we have never seen such perfectly clean murders. It defies logic."

"I can't understand it", said Kenneth shaking his head. "Now Chief, you said there was a second anomaly."

"Yes. At the beginning of this interview, you said that a young blonde secretary greeted you in the ante-room of the Chancellor's suite. Do you wish to re-consider that statement?"

"No Chief I would not", said Kenneth rather indignantly. "I am telling you the truth".

"Had you ever seen this young lady before?"

"No".

"Did you know that the Chancellor's secretary was a middle aged dark complexioned woman?"

"I had only once been to the Chancellor's office. And that was over four years ago. I can't remember all these details".

"The *real* Chancellor's secretary was found murdered. Her body was hanging in the large cupboard at the back of her work area."

Kent stared at Kenneth for a moment. The young man was ashen-faced.

"Then who was this young woman who greeted me", he asked

"Exactly our question", snapped the Chief.

"It would seem most unlikely that this young woman would have the strength to commit these horrific murders."

"Indeed not. It is more likely that she was an accomplice of some kind".

King's College University was like a war zone. The areas around the Chancellor's offices and the Department of Physics were cordoned off and swarming with police and press. Apart from the Department of Physics, life at the rest of the University had to go on as best as possible. Until a new Head was appointed, all teaching and research activities had been suspended.

A few days after these dreadful happenings Kenneth and Hilary were strolling through the campus grounds discussing the fast turn of events.

"The Chancellor, two faculty and two secretaries all murdered. What exactly is the link? After all there are plenty of 'non-orthodox' people around who spout their politically incorrect views far more vociferously than those four had ever done. Why not murder more prominent types? Surely it would make better sense to assassinate high profile politicians than obscure academics." So reasoned Kenneth as he walked with his girl-friend around the campus.

"Apart from criticizing the wackier sides of PC like your green cheese moon", said Hilary almost bursting out laughing, "these four victims, at least as far as I know, were pretty much apolitical".

"It's beyond comprehension – is all I can really say", answered Kenneth. He knew perfectly well that he was lying to his girlfriend. He knew that he was the common thread that linked these murders. They were all people he knew or had associations with.

CHAPTER 8.
More Bizarre Events.

As winter rolled into spring and spring into summer, the murders stopped. However, more faculty at the University appeared to be succumbing to politically correct ideology.

Many students throughout the University also started to re-arrange their patterns of political thinking in favour of the absurd reasoning associated with PC. Douglas Randal, a third year student majoring in Geography was one of those who had 'seen the darkness' as Kenneth liked to put it.

"You used to be so full of common sense in your ways of thinking Doug", said Kenneth one day as they were sitting having a beer in a pub near the University. "Why the change, Doug?"

"Well, so many people are coming round to the politically correct way of thinking. Can all these people be wrong?"

"Doug, at one time only a tiny handful of people believed the Earth was a globe and that it circled the sun. Were they wrong? Was the vast majority right?"

"But the majority soon accepted the views of the minority. The same process is happening. At one time PCism was held by a small elite minority."

"It still is".

"Yes, but that minority is fast becoming a largish minority. The next stage will be that PCism will be accepted by the majority as the only legitimate form of political expression".

"Majorities do not make truth Doug, no matter by what process majority opinion is arrived at. It is evidence that makes the truth".

Douglas Randal just sighed. He struck Kenneth as being extremely tired. He stared past Kenneth with that far away look in his eyes.

Later in the evening of the same day that Kenneth had had that strange conversation with his friend Douglas Randal, Kenneth and Hilary were emerging from King's College University's main library. As they walked towards their accommodation, they noticed two familiar figures at the corner of the street. Roger Edmore and his girlfriend Patricia Towler were standing staring up at the sky.

"Anything interesting up there Rog?" Kenneth asked his friend cheerily.

Roger and Patricia just kept gazing up into the sky. It was Patricia who gave the answer. "Haven't you seen them Kenneth? What about you Hilary?"

"Seen what?" Hilary asked.

Roger and Patricia now lowered their upturned heads and gazed upon Kenneth and Hilary with glassy looking eyes.

"They beamed us up Ken", Roger informed his friend. "They conducted experiments on us".

Roger and Patricia continued to have that distant look in their eyes. Kenneth's mind went back to his pub conversation with Doug Randal.

"Good God man!" exclaimed Kenneth shaking Roger by the shoulders. "Are you all right?"

"Patricia dear", said Hilary. "What's going on?"

"We now know better", said Roger. "We were in error when we were politically incorrect".

"You both need to see a doctor", commented Hilary.

"And pronto", added Kenneth.

"Leave us Kenneth, leave us Hilary, leave us with our newly found love – our love of Political Correctness".

"Come on", Kenneth said to Hilary.

"What the hell is going on?" said Kenneth to Hilary as they left their friends who just kept gazing up into the sky. He then told Hilary about the chat he had had earlier in the day with Douglas Randal.

"A few of my friends have seemingly gone gaga too", replied Hilary. "All seem to want to bear witness to the validity of Political Correctness".

"I want to get to the bottom of all this nonsense", said Kenneth. "But how? That's the big problem. How?!"

Kenneth floundered into his bed and sank into a deep sleep. At 3am he was awoken by his telephone. It was Hilary.

"Kenneth, Kenneth", she stammered.

"Hilary! Is everything all right?"

"Kenneth, I, I just…. I just wanted to tell you that… well that, we ought to be politically correct. We, we, you know, I mean….we can't go on resisting it you know Kenneth".

"Hilary, what's happening to you?" shouted Kenneth down the phone.

"Nothing, nothing. It's just that….it's nothing just that…oh I think I'm going to be sick. My head is light and…"

The phone went silent. Hilary had not hung up, there was still a connection, but Hilary failed to respond to Kenneth's questions.

"Hilary, Hilary!" Kenneth yelled. "Are you still there?"

Kenneth only heard her heavy breathing. It was clear that she had fainted. He quickly dressed and rushed round to her flat. He banged hard on the door but there was no answer. When in frustration he tried the handle, he discovered that the door was locked. With his shoulder, he forced open the door, rushed in and found Hilary lying on the floor unconscious beside the phone. He quickly replaced the receiver. He cradled Hilary in his arms. She regained consciousness a little. She opened her eyes and Kenneth could see the same glassy far off look he had noticed in the eyes of Douglas, Roger and Patricia. He rushed to the phone and called an ambulance.

"You'd might as well move your lodgings to this police station, Mr. Mackenzie", said Tony Kent.

"I'm in and out of this place like a yoyo. Do you have any idea what is going on?"

"We're as much in the dark as you are sir".

"I've told you all I know. May I go now? I want to see Hilary?"

"Sorry Mr. Mackenzie but we have obtained a district magistrate's warrant to prevent anyone from seeing her until we formally and officially interview her."

"This is surely not normal procedure".

"We are in very abnormal times."

"When can I see her?"

"After we have interviewed her".

"When will that be?"

"When the hospital inform us that she is strong enough to give one?"

Back at his flat, an exhausted Kenneth Mackenzie picked up his phone and wearily dialed Halifax Central Hospital. He was curtly told by the ward sister that there was to be a total blackout on information until the police had interviewed Hilary. Three days went by and Mackenzie was summoned to the police station.

"So, how is she? That is – if I may ask".

"She's fine answered Kent".

"Can you shed any light on what happened to her?"

"Before I answer that question, let me ask you this: did you smell any gas when you entered Hilary's flat?"

"Let me think", said Kenneth. "If I did I wouldn't probably have noticed. My concern was for Hilary, not gas!"

"I understand that", Kent said somewhat impatiently. "But think back to the time and think hard."

After about thirty seconds of deep thought, Kenneth replied.

"Yes", he suddenly said. "Now that I think about it, there was a slight smell of gas".

"Thank you", was all the Police Chief's reply.

"So was it some gas then that put her into this condition?"

"Exactly."

"Well, I'm mystified as to where the gas came from as Hilary is all electric".

"So are we Mr. Mackenzie, but there's more. We're also mystified about the cocaine that was found in her blood."

"Oh!" cried out Kenneth. "Then I'm convinced she was the victim of foul play. Hilary is simply not a drug addict –never, never".

"As policemen we have to consider all possibilities. However we did find heroine and cocaine hidden under her bed. I'm sorry sir, but the facts are the facts."

"Well, I'm convinced they were planted there."

"We consider that as a strong possibility. However, as professional policemen, we cannot let emotion creep into our investigations."

"I *know* that Hilary is not the sort of person who deals in narcotics."

"Perhaps not. But there's more still."

"What?"

"The hospital found a strange substance in her blood. It has never been isolated before. The toxicologists are mystified."

Kenneth looked very serious and thoughtful. "Did she say anything about being abducted by aliens – I mean, taken on board an alien spacecraft?

Kent looked incredulously at Mackenzie. "What?" he simply said.

"That is exactly my question Chief".

"I'm not sure who is being more absurd – you or Hilary".

"Chief Kent, you said that as a professional policeman, you were bound to consider all possibilities in an objective and dispassionate manner, am I right?"

"Yes".

"And did you not also say that we are living in somewhat peculiar times with peculiar happenings?"

"Yes", was again the Police Chief's reply.

"Then, with respect to you, Mr. Kent, may I ask you to practice what you preach."

"Well, Mr. Mackenzie", said the Chief, straightening himself up and puffing out his chest, "if you are asking me to start chasing flying saucers and little green men, then you are asking me to waste police time. You may believe in UFOs, but I'm a rational man, Mr. Mackenzie – so, quite simply, I don't!"

"Police Chief Kent", said Kenneth gritting his teeth. "I am not asking you to chase UFOs; in fact, I am not even asking you to believe in them. And, furthermore, I never said that I believed in them myself – to be frank, I don't."

"Then sir, what exactly are you getting at? Could you please come to the point?"

Kenneth Mackenzie then related to the Chief the scene where he and Hilary saw their two friends Roger Edmore and Patricia Towler gazing up into the night sky.

"Now I'm not saying", continued Kenneth, "that there are actually alien spacecraft. However, I have been checking the internet and have noticed that there have, over the past few months, been a surge in abduction claims and reports of UFO sightings."

"I still don't see what you are getting at", commented Kent rather impatiently.

"My belief is this", said Mackenzie taking a deep breath, "is that someone, or some organisation is using a psychedelic drug to create these hallucinations".

"That is a fairly rational analysis", said the police chief, "but I'm not convinced".

"I don't mean to tell you how to do your job, Mr. Kent, but may I suggest you contact your colleagues in the areas where UFOs have been spotted and ask if there are weird stories about abductions and/or narcotic substances found in the blood of drugged victims".

"It's a reasonable line of enquiry, Mr. Mackenzie, but I'll have to think how I'm going to approach my counterparts without appearing to them as someone having flipped my lid".

"Also, this unknown narcotic substance could well be the means by which brain chemistry is altered to make the mind 'politically correct', if that doesn't seem too far fetched."

"Now here's my question. Why is it that some people are murdered and some are drugged? Is there a pattern here?"

"Off-hand, I can't think of one".

"Neither can I?"

A week later, Kenneth Mackenzie got a 'phone call. It was Hilary.

"Oh Hilary dear, you're home. I'm coming round right away."

When Kenneth got to Hilary's flat, he asked her exactly what had happened.

"Someone came up behind me while I was sitting at the fire reading. This man pushed a nozzle on my mouth and gave me a doze of gas. This instantly caused me to faint. When I awoke, there were puncture marks in my arm. He had injected something into me."

"How though did the assailant gain entry to your flat? There are no signs of forced entry either by door or windows."

"It's a mystery both to me and even to the police".

"Hilary. Why don't you take the flat across the landing from mine? At least I'll be near you."

"Yes Ken. It's a good idea."

Kenneth then told Hilary about his theories regarding the gas and the strange narcotic substance.

"But you know Ken, I'm still, well, politically incorrect, in a manner of speaking and I have had no abduction experiences – real or imaginary".

"It seems your mind is made of tougher stuff. However, whoever tried this may try again with an even stronger dose."

"I've got some interesting news for you", said Tony Kent to Kenneth Mackenzie on the 'phone. "Could you come to the police station now?

"Sure. I'm on my way".

When Kenneth entered the police chief's office, Kent was sitting at his desk shuffling through a pile of papers. He looked up after a few seconds and beckoned his visitor to a seat.

"My apologies to you Mr. Mackenzie for doubting your analysis. Take a read through these reports".

For five minutes Kenneth studied the reports. They were from the police authorities.

"It seems like my theory is corroborated. In the parts of Canada where drug addiction has been on the increase there is a correlation between the intake of narcotic substances, UFO sightings - and Political Correctness."

"Yes", said the Chief nodding his head.

"But who is behind it? They must be very subtle operators. Look at the way they gained entry into Hilary's flat".

"All I can say sir is that my men and I are doing our utmost to solve this riddle".

Hilary moved into the flat near Kenneth's. She felt more secure being near her boyfriend.

One evening she and Kenneth were sitting in her flat and discussing the issue of global warming.

"I'm not a scientist Ken, but isn't it the consensus among the scientific community that global warming is a fact and that it is being caused by carbon emissions."

"If you watch the television and read the newspapers, you'll notice that those who speak about global warming are mainly politicians, diplomats and journalists. Real scientists pooh pooh the whole idea."

"And yet", said Hilary very thoughtfully, "I have seen some scientists being interviewed on telly who do go along with anthropogenic global warming."

"Yes, I know that. However, when you examine carefully who those scientists are, they are working in establishments which are financed by government grants. So they have to watch their jobs and play the PC game. I really don't think they believe any of the nonsense they come away with."

"So why do governments want us to swallow whole all this garbage about global warming?"

"It's social control. They want us to believe that only supranational and international organisations are capable of dealing with something which transcends national boundaries."

"So it's a mechanism for advancing the New World Order – a One World Government?"

"Spot on".

"So what is the scientific rationale behind the rejection of man-made global warming?"

"Well, first of all, the Earth's climate has always been changing. We've had a number of ice ages and we've had times when crocodiles, tigers and elephants roamed near the poles. Now there is no way that these extremes of temperature and climate change could have come about through human agencies."

"And isn't it the case that carbon dioxide is only a trace gas in the atmosphere?"

"Indeed it is. It constitutes only around 0.02% of the gases of which our atmosphere is composed. So CO2 cannot be the vehicle for any global warming that is occurring. And also there is the question as to what is cause and what is effect. Do increases in CO2 cause temperature increase or does temperature increase lead to an increase in the incidence of CO2?"

"So what could be the reason for temperature fluctuations?"

"It is a very complex issue. Sun-spot activity, variations in solar radiation output, even our position in the galaxy."

"But isn't our position in the galaxy fixed?"

"No, not at all. The galaxy rotates around its centre."

"But doesn't CO2 trap radiation?"

"Yes of course. Thank goodness it does or we'd all freeze to death. And CO2 isn't the only greenhouse gas. Water vapour, nitrous oxide, methane, ozone and chlorofluorocarbons are other gases which produce the greenhouse effect. Carbon dioxide comes a poor second after water vapour as a greenhouse gas. Water vapour contributes between 36 – 72% of the greenhouse effect, CO2 between 9 and 26%. Methane is between 4 – 9% and Ozone between 3 – 7%."

"And I suppose CO_2 is vital for plants?"

"Absolutely." Kenneth looked very thoughtful for a moment. "Hilary?", he eventually said in a questioning tone.

"Yes Ken", she replied rather tensely.

"Hilary, there's something I've been meaning to ask you for some time now".

"What is it Ken?" said Hilary noticing the slight trembling in her boyfriend's voice.

"Hilary. Will you marry me?" said Kenneth falling down in front of her on one knee.

Hilary threw back her head in laughter and replied, "yes of course Ken, of course".

CHAPTER 9.
Out Of This World.

Kenneth Mackenzie had difficulty getting to sleep that night. He was so excited at the thought of being wed to Hilary. He thought about the future, about a home, about children. At length, Kenneth settled down and started to doze off. All of a sudden he was awakened by a scream from Hilary's flat. He jumped out of bed and ran across the landing and banged on Hilary's door. The screaming continued and Kenneth heard the sound of violent struggling going on. He tried the door and found it to be open. He dashed in and saw Hilary bruised and bloodied beside a table in her living-room. Behind him he heard the sound of someone rushing out of the door. He turned round and saw a masked man dash from the flat. Kenneth pursued Hilary's assailant downstairs. It was too late; the man jumped on a motorcycle and sped off. Kenneth ran back upstairs.

"It's lucky you didn't sleep well last night, Mr. Mackenzie. It's obvious that whoever broke into your fiancé's flat intended to murder her", said Tony Kent in solemn tones.

"How is she now?"

"Hospital says she'll be OK in a day or so. She's suffering from shock more than from physical injuries."

"I'm beginning to see another piece of the jigsaw in this puzzle".

"Which is?"

"Murders occur on second or higher floors while gassings and druggings occur at ground floor level."

"OK – but what is that supposed to mean?"

"I don't know. But it is something to bear in mind while you are pursuing your enquiries Chief."

"Yeah, well... yeah", responded the Chief in a rather unconvinced way.

"Anyway, I want to go to the hospital and see Hilary. Right now, she is my main concern".

"Sure – yeah, of course, eh sure".

Kenneth walked out of the police station and made his way towards the hospital. He saw Hilary and was pleased with her progress. Sitting beside her hospital bed and holding her hand in his, he said, "Hilary, the sooner we're married the better. You'll be beside me and I'll be better able to protect you."

"Yes Ken", replied Hilary, looking lovingly into Kenneth's eyes. "The doctors think I'll be fit enough to be discharged in a couple of days. We'll start planning for the wedding."

"That'll give us both something to look forward to".

That same evening, Kenneth was walking back from his laboratory towards his flat. It was dark and he had the uneasy feeling that he was being followed. He looked around but saw nothing. He started walking again, but the uneasy feeling of being watched persisted. When he got to his flat, he cautiously looked around before applying the key to the door-lock. He walked into his flat and closed the door. Before he could turn on the light, he was pounced on by three men. They wore stockings over their faces so Kenneth could not see them. Instantly a nozzle was pushed over his mouth. Kenneth struggled as hard as he could but the gas was applied and he passed out.

Kenneth came to very slowly. His head felt heavy and his body felt weak. He was lying on some kind of bed. It was quite comfortable. After about fifteen or twenty minutes later, Kenneth started to feel better. He was strong enough to stand on his feet. He got off the bed and started to examine his surroundings. There was a DVD monitor with a wide selection of DVDs in the cabinet underneath it. Not far from it was a CD player with a selection of different types of music on CDs next to it. There was a toilet off the room with shower facility. And of course there was the inevitable computer. All seemed quite normal except for one thing – the room had no windows.

"Strange", he thought. "I'm still politically incorrect. And it seems my captors want to make me feel as comfortable as possible. Yet they don't want me to see where exactly I am."

Kenneth noticed that the room had no door. There looked like some sort of entranceway that seemed like the automatic parting doors of a lift, but when Kenneth went over to them, they just simply remained closed.

"Well, I suppose all will be revealed sooner or later", thought the distraught young man.

He decided to freshen himself up. He had a shower and a shave and then proceeded to brush his teeth. Everything had been provided for his creature comforts. It appeared he had the best of everything.

When Kenneth dried himself, he came through to the main room, dressed himself in some new clothes which had been provided by his generous assailants and jailers. Suddenly he heard a kind of droning sound behind him. A part of the wall was opening up. Kenneth walked over to it and saw to his amazement it contained a small slim shaped glass. He sniffed it and realised it was a liqueur of some sort. At first he was a little suspicious but then he decided to drink it.

"They're not going to provide all these facilities and then poison me", he thought. So he drank the liqueur and found it had no adverse effects.

Then a light flashed on a small rectangular panel near the dumb waiter. A notice was displayed which stated Please Replace The Glass. Kenneth did so and the automatic doors of the dumb waiter closed. About thirty seconds later they opened again and revealed a plate of delicious smelling hot scotch broth. The same procedure was repeated and the next course of turkey with all the trimmings was served up. A bottle of Cabarnet Sauvignon was provided to accompany the meal. Chocolate cake, coffee and a cognac rounded off the meal.

At last the 'lift looking doors' parted. Kenneth stiffened, not really knowing what or who to expect. Yet, no-one and nothing emerged. Kenneth slowly walked towards them. Another room was revealed. It was a fully equipped gymnasium. Kenneth walked around the fitness room and examined all the exercise contraptions.

"Mmmm", he thought. "Well, it looks like they want me to keep myself in good shape. But why, why, why?" he said out loud. "What is all this about?"

In the bed-sit part of this complex, he heard a beeping sound. He went through to investigate. It was the computer monitor. A message came up which read: "Please make yourself at home. Prepare yourself to be here for the next three months".

For three whole months Kenneth did just that. He really had no choice in the matter. Every day he worked out, ate his meals, watched DVDs, listened to music, read and studied.

After three long months Kenneth sat expectantly at his desk. Behind him he heard a hissing sound. He spun round and saw the walls on the far end of room starting to open. Two people – a man and a woman – entered the room. They were dressed in silvery boiler suit type outfits. Kenneth guessed that they were engineers or technicians of some sort.

The man wasted no time with social formalities. "Herr Mackenzie, vill you please be so kind as to come zis vay?"

Kenneth's heart sank. "Oh dear!" he thought. "I've been captured by the Fourth Reich brigade".

Outside of his place of confinement, Kenneth walked along a number of corridors. The whole of the place exuded an ultra-modern air.

"Where am I?" Kenneth asked.

The two people accompanying him made no reply.

About three minutes later, Kenneth and his dour companions came to a halt outside some auto-doors. These opened and revealed a massive room full of scientists, technicians, and computer equipment. The man and the woman accompanied Kenneth to a chair where a man was sitting working on something which looked like some highly advanced computer.

"Herr Mackenzie is here sir", said the woman.

The man on the chair stood up and faced Mackenzie.

"You!" Kenneth blurted out. It was Tony Kent, the Halifax police chief!

"I always thought I could trust you. Now I can see that you're part of this whole criminal network".

"Don't jump to conclusions so quickly my man", said Kent somewhat harshly. "All will be revealed to you – at the appropriate time."

"And where am I? What is going on here?"

"I will show you where you are Kenneth. Look over there at the screen - but steel yourself for a bit of a shock".

Kenneth just stood agape at what he saw. It was the red planet – Mars.

"So – so, so this, this is…" stuttered Kenneth.

"This is a spaceship", said Kent quite calmly.

Kenneth stood speechless for a good two minutes. He stared at the screen mesmerised by the red glow of Mars.

"In another two days we will be in low orbit over Mars. Be patient Kenneth more will be revealed to you".

"If you think I'm going to co-operate with the crooked activities of a bent copper, you're sadly mistaken."

"You'll be happy to co-operate with us Kenneth. And we're not asking you to do anything for 'bent coppers'".

"Who really are you? And what precisely is your game?" said Kenneth angrily.

"In good time Kenneth – all in good time. Enough for now." Turning to the two escorts, Kent ordered them to take Kenneth back to his quarters.

Two days later the craft was, as Kent had said, in low orbit over Mars. Kenneth was taken by his escorts to the craft's control room.

"Kenneth", said Tony Kent, "this is Commander David Wilson, the Captain of this ship."

Kenneth shook hands with the Wilson who seemed to be a pleasant enough chap.

"I want you to observe the terrain over which we are currently flying", said Wilson. "Have you any idea as to what these features are?" asked Wilson pointing to the large monitor.

"They are the mysterious glass worms or glass tubes which unmanned spacecraft have photographed over the past few decades."

"And what do you know about them?"

"Nothing. All sorts of strange theories are associated with them. Some people have said that they are mysterious forms of life, others that they are the remains of a lost Martian civilisation. And in any case Captain, I'm not into playing guessing games. If you know anything about them or anything else, just tell me plainly."

"In due course", was all that Wilson said in reply.

"I won't hold my breath", said Mackenzie sneeringly.

The following day the craft landed on the red planet. Mackenzie was directed to don a spacesuit and life support equipment.

Mackenzie, Kent, Wilson and the twenty crew members assembled in the main bay area of the craft. The main hatch opened to reveal a bleak, cold, windswept and rock strewn Martian landscape. They walked outside to a balcony like contraption. Once there, the contraption descended to the Martian surface. Mackenzie looked around at the desolate landscape. He gazed upon the mysterious ship that had brought him to Mars. It was shaped like a flying saucer. He noticed the lights on the outside of the craft dim slowly. Commander

Wilson told everyone that it would be a very long time before they would ever need this craft again. Kenneth thought about his parents and he thought about Hilary.

"Will I ever see my Mum and Dad again? And Hilary?" he thought to himself.

For around fifteen minutes the twenty two Earthlings stood on the Martian surface. Kenneth thought again about the craft which had taken him on his three month journey to the red planet. His mind went back to the time when he and Hilary heard the story from their friends Roger Edmore and Patricia Towler of how they had been abducted and taken on board an alien spacecraft. Perhaps it wasn't hallucinogens after all. Yet, the people on the craft he had just spent three months in were real flesh and blood human beings.

Far off in the distance, Kenneth thought he saw what looked like a vehicle coming towards them. In ten minutes it came close enough for him to discern the shape of a bus – but a bus which had no wheels. Like a hovercraft it floated about three feet above the surface of the planet.

Eventually the strange vehicle came to a halt about 50 feet from the craft and its doors opened. Everyone was directed by David Wilson to enter. When all 22 were on the bus, the doors closed and the bus started its journey across the Martian plain.

"You may take off your pressure suits", the driver of the bus told his passengers.

Kenneth was glad to get out of that uncomfortable clothing. He looked out of the window and observed that the bus was making its way to some massive glass domed structures.

"These must be the 'glass worms'", thought Kenneth.

The bus drew up alongside one of the massive domes. A long rectangular like structure moved out from the side of the bus facing the dome. The inside doors of the bus opened on to the inside of this structure and the passengers were directed to enter. Once inside the doors of the bus closed behind them and the doors in front of the structure opened up.

"Please proceed inside", came the bus driver's German accented voice over the intercom.

The inside looked like a large railway station. It was full of platforms, rails and signaling devices. Soon a long train whizzed to a halt in front of the party. All were directed to board and to remove any fears they might still be harbouring regarding all that they had seen and experienced on the Martian surface.

The train sped off at high speed. Sometimes it was above ground and sometimes below ground – but always within the glassy structures. Now Kenneth knew that these glass tubes were indeed artificial. So far though everyone seemed very human – so far, no little green men.

At last they came to a halt at a very large platform. Everyone alighted from the train and the massive platform started to descend. For ten minutes the platform made its slow descent to a depth of around 300 feet. When the large platform came to a halt, Mackenzie was astonished to see before him a huge city. The city was bathed in a soft white light that seemed to come from every place.

"This is Radiant City", Kent told Mackenzie. It is six miles in diameter. It has everything you would find in a city back on Earth – except weather".

"So who built this city? What is it all about?"

Tony Kent and David Wilson simply guided Mackenzie to a small car-like vehicle.

"The City Director will answer all your questions", said Wilson.

CHAPTER 10.
Mars Bar.

The three drove along a wide open highway. It was the most beautiful city which Kenneth had ever seen. It was clean, in fact it was clinically clean. The houses were well proportioned and well spaced out. Children played in the parks which were full of trees, lakes and gardens. There was no pollution of any sort. Wilson explained that all power was nuclear generated. Even the car was run on a tiny micro-chip nuclear cell which lasted on average up to three years.

"This must be the nearest one can get to a Garden of Eden this side of eternity", thought Kenneth.

At length the car stopped outside a very smart looking restaurant. The establishment was in fact a combined restaurant and bar. Wilson asked the waiter for a table for four.

"Let's have a drink while we're waiting for the City Director", said David Wilson.

Kenneth was astonished to find that all the brand labels on the various bottles were exactly the same as those on Earth.

"Most of the plonk is locally made", explained Kent. "Only pricey places like this have the Earth stuff. We bring back crate-loads of it during our Earth-Mars runs".

As they were sipping away at their drinks, the waiter directed a middle-aged bespectacled man to their table. Everyone immediately stood up. Kent and Wilson exchanged greetings with the man.

"Kenneth, this is Dr. Rudolph Von Hildeger", said David Wilson.

The two men shook hands.

"Please be seated gentlemen", said Von Hildeger. "I hope you had a pleasant enough trip to Mars, Kenneth".

"Yes, but I really must ask for an explanation as to what all this is about".

"It's a long story Kenneth. Or eh – I should say 'Sir Kenneth'".

Kenneth was agape.

"We know all about you, Sir Kenneth. And all about what happened in Bruce's Cave", continued Von Hildeger. "Please bear with me Sir Kenneth as I tell you everything. As I say, it's a long story".

"I'm listening", said Kenneth, "but the story had better be good".

"As you know, Hitler and some highly trained scientists, engineers and other professional people escaped from the Bunker in 1945".

"I know that", said Kenneth somewhat impatiently.

"What you don't know is this: the descendants of Hitler and his henchmen all live in underground dwellings on Earth. They have succeeded in manufacturing a narcotic agent which in combination with methane gas causes a change in the brain chemistry and neurological networking to create a politically correct mind-set."

"I had already figured that out. But you, and this whole Martian complex. Whose side are you on? Is this an extension of what is going on back on Earth?"

Von Hildeger took a deep breath and sat back in his chair, thus conveying to Kenneth to prepare himself for a long explanation.

"Before, during and after the war, Hitler's supporters and their succeeding generations built a network of underground tunnels which now stretch around the globe. These lead off from the underground dwelling compounds and terminate at government ministries, commercial company HQs, colleges and universities and various other key establishments. In fact, they can lead into the very hearths and homes of people. That is how your fiancé was drugged. You wondered why the drugging happens at ground floor level. There is your answer. Murders occur where the tunnels cannot reach – first floor levels and above."

"How do you know all this?" asked Kenneth rather suspiciously.

"You will no doubt have noticed that there is a preponderance of Germans here."

"Yes", said Kenneth, again rather suspiciously.

"You see Kenneth, not all Germans were Nazi supporters during the Second World War. Those who were well educated did not go along with the sort of racial and other nonsense spoken by Hitler and his cohorts."

"Well", interrupted Kenneth, "what about all those scientists who escaped with Hitler and who, along with their descendants, have caused so much havoc?"

"They were not the best", Von Hildeger answered. "You will no doubt have heard of Dr. Wernher Von Braun, the German rocket scientist who developed the V1 and V2 bombs at Peenemunde in northern Germany."

"I have indeed", said Kenneth.

"Apart from his official research into and subsequent development of these rocket missiles, Dr. Von Braun and many of his colleagues were working according to a secret agenda."

"Which was?"

"Nothing less than space travel. You see the Nazis had started their tunneling and underground networks way back in the early 1930's. It was a precautionary measure, an insurance policy if you like, in case of defeat. Von Braun knew about this and he and like-minded intellectuals decided to do something to counteract this. Nazi scientists were highly advanced in the use and manipulation of gas – not surprising of course considering that they had gassed six million Jews. Using a sophisticated process involving gas and narcotics, they devised this drug which would attack the logical and reasoning functions of the brain – hence political correctness and all its illogicality and irrationality. Combining this with some very clever politics which on the surface were 'anti-Nazi' and 'left-wing', Hitler and his cohorts continued the war by subtle means using the gas-drug combination via the subterranean networks."

"What about the so-called UFO sightings? Where do they all fit in?"

"Von Braun and other scientists were also working on craft capable of vertical take-off. Runways of course are impossible underground. So the Vertical Take-off Flying Craft was invented. This is why it was in the immediate post-war period that reports of UFOs, flying saucers and alien abductions so dramatically increased. The abductions were real enough – but they were conducted by flesh and blood humans – well, in as much as we could ever call the Nazis 'human'. As you will doubtless know, abductees invariably spoke about being experimented on and anatomically examined. This was simply a continuation of the Nazis' evil policy of human experimentation."

"What was the purpose of these experiments?"

"It was to test more advanced drug formulas. Another purpose of the VTFCs was for the collection of narcotics cargo. Their sole supplier is a Columbian drug baron."

"So he is part of the Nazi network?"

"No. He doesn't know anything about it. He doesn't care. The Nazis are his best customers and he's only interested in the money. His contact man is a certain Herr Mulinger. As Mulinger and his Nazi bosses don't want to associate the drug consignments with the VTFCs, Mulinger uses a twin engine plane to come from and go to the poppy plantation. Pedro Gonzagos, the owner, built a short runway outside of his plantation especially for Mulinger's plane. The narcotics are loaded onto the plane; once air-borne, the cargo is transferred to the waiting VTFC and the plane is destroyed. The Nazis give Gonzagos enough money to buy another plane for each consignment. Scattered around the world on high mountain tops and other unknown locations, are the secret entrance-ways to the Nazi's underground complexes".

"How is all of this financed?"

"Mainly through the sale of illegal drugs on the Black Market. However, Nazi gold and numbered Swiss bank accounts are also part of the financing process. The Nazis also have their underground printing presses where they churn out forged bank notes. Another source of finance comes from the government of Saudi Arabia. As you know, the appeasement of extremist Islam has been a major plank in the politically correct movement. Because of their policy of exterminating the Jews, Hitler and the Nazi regime have always been great hits with the Saudis. So the Saudi regime has consistently worked to undermine the national security of countries around the world".

"Now how does this tie in with the craft which brought me to Mars?"

"As I told you earlier, Wernher Von Braun and his colleagues had a hidden agenda. They produced a VTFC model for the Nazis – but, they had secretly designed far more advanced models which were capable of inter-planetary flight. These designs were never shown to the upper echelons of the Nazi regime."

"So why come to Mars, why not simply tell the victorious allies about Hitler's secret plans?"

"Even a genius like Von Braun would have been passed off as a lunatic and a crank. No-one would have believed him. And if the Nazis ever had any inkling that their plans were known, I mean, if their underground activities had become public rumour, they would have probably operated a Plan B which may have been to move even deeper underground or resort to some desperate measure like the use of atomic weapons. The allies only beat them to developing the A Bomb by a whisker's breadth. So we were sure they had the technology."

"So what happened then?"

"We realised that we would have to continue the fight outside of the Earth. We used robots to build the first above-ground domed habitable structure on Mars in 1944. Von Braun controlled the entire operation from Peenemunde. When the structure was up and functioning, masses of men and materials were sent to Mars to construct the kind of underground cities you now see. Over the past 80 years, we have built a complex of twenty-five underground cities. The capital is called Cydonia City and is a massive twenty miles in diameter."

"So what people interpreted as intelligent life on Mars when they examined the photographs of 'glass tubes' or sometimes named 'glass worms' was in fact your construction projects".

"Precisely".

"What about the Face on Mars and the various other 'monuments' like pyramids and temples of which Richard Hoagland and others wrote?"

"These were all decoys built by our engineers. For security reasons, we wanted to convey the impression of a long-lost Martian civilization."

"Why construct the cities underground?"

"For two reasons. First of all as a protection against dangerous radiation and secondly from attack. Had the Nazis ever found out about our Marian bases, they may have developed and launched missiles capable of reaching Mars."

"They may still do so", Mackenzie warned Von Hildeger.

"True – but we are safer deep underground. Furthermore, we have constructed a missile defence system to intercept any incoming missiles. Hopefully they won't be needed – but they are an added insurance policy."

"This whole Mars operation which you have just described reminds me of a certain Dr. Ernest L. Norman who, while in deep meditation, went on a mystical astral flight to Mars and was shown things rather similar to what you have constructed here. His guide was a supposed Martian named Nur El."

"Dr. Norman was a brilliant physicist. He was one of us. His trips to Mars were wide awake tangible events. He helped with the construction of the cities. He made his first journey here in 1955."

"So why did he write in such mystical ways and describe his journeys here as astral events while in a meditative state of mind?"

"He couldn't state openly what was actually going on".

"Why write about it at all then?"

"For those who would be intelligent enough to read below the surface narrative".

"And were there any who did?"

"Unfortunately none. However, we have here the off-spring of all the brilliant minds who came to Mars at the end of the Second World War. Although most are of German descent, we have many who came from Britain, America, India, Africa and China. Kenneth, we are the *real* anti-Nazis."

"So what exactly do the Nazis want to do on Earth now?

"They are on the verge of winning World War II. In fact, I'd say that they have already won it. They will stand up in the United Nations, Europe and a host of other international organisations and declare a One World Government. If the useful idiots like Benson, Morrison and Davidson don't die of shock once they realise what suckers they have been, they will probably be given lethal doses. People like Flora Fraser who simply pretend to be politically correct will perhaps either continue the pretence out of pure self-preservation instincts or form clandestine resistance movements. But they will be futile. The useful idiots will be eliminated as their drug drenched brains are now so frazzled and fried that they could never function in a post-politically correct society. Those whose brains have been altered to the state of mediocrity will become a sort of drone class doing the sort of humdrum jobs that pigeons could perform. The top jobs in government, bureaucracy, and science will go to the Nazis whose brains, though of evil slant, are nevertheless in pristine condition".

"Now", said Kenneth in a somewhat firm tone of voice, "why did you bring me to this planet the way you did? Couldn't you have told me all of this on Earth?"

"We brought you here because of your scientific know-how and to protect you from the catastrophe which will soon hit the Earth. In the more immediate term, your life was in danger. Sooner or later, you would have gone the way of the Chancellor, Carpenter, Artcliff and the others"

"But why with such violence? Why did you drug me? Why all the secrecy until now?

"You may not have believed us. You perhaps would have been suspicious of our motives. If you had refused to come after our explaining all this to you, you would have constituted a weak link in our security. In other words, you might have spoken to the wrong people about our Mars operations. We couldn't take that chance."

"All right. I understand. Now I noticed that there was normal gravity on the craft which carried me here."

"We have devised ways to create artificial gravity. That is a technicality you don't need to know about at this stage. In the meantime – let's eat."

"How exactly do you obtain your food and water?"

"We have farms both above ground (under protective domes) and the newer more advanced agriculture and horticultural areas below ground."

"And air?"

"From water by electrolysis."

"And the water?"

"A number of ways. From reservoirs at the Poles. We drain off the little water there which is mixed with frozen Carbon Dioxide. We tap underground rivers and lakes. Also, we are perfecting a process of synthetically manufacturing water from other elements."

"A very important question I must ask. Do you know anything about my parents? What happened to them? And what about my fiancé Hilary Jennings".

"I can tell you about them later Kenneth, later", was all Rudolph Von Hildeger's reply.

CHAPTER 11.
Apophis.

"What exactly do you want me to do here?" Kenneth asked Von Hildeger as he drove him to his accommodation after taking leave of David Wilson and Tony Kent.

"Although we have been on Mars for around 80 years, we have never viewed our presence here as permanent. The one hundred thousand of us who now live here still see Earth as the 'home planet'". We are a 'happy family' here Kenneth. We have no politics, no factionalism and no religious bigotry and hatred. In this sense, we do see ourselves as a, a, eh dare I say it, 'master race', but not in the sense that the Nazis or the politically correct would understand the term. So most of us do not want to return to the pollution (I mean social and political pollution) of the Earth. Everyone here now is fifth and six generation. Mars has always been their world. Yet not one of us, nay, not one has ever forgotten our raison d'etre for being here – to eventually liberate the Earth from the Nazis. It has been the dream that has kept us sane on this barren planet. It has been the goal for which we have never ceased to strive."

"What exactly is your point, Dr. Von Hildeger?" asked Kenneth rather impatiently.

"I'm just coming to it. The core research project which has been going on here for nearly 80 years is to develop an anti-dote to the gas/drug combination being used by the Nazis, and…."

"And after eight decades you still can't produce one" interrupted Kenneth.

"Sir Kenneth Mackenzie", said Von Hildeger rather indignantly, "it has not been easy to find samples of this substance or to obtain blood samples from victims."

"I understand", replied Kenneth rather apologetically.

"Nevertheless, the perseverance and hard work of our scientists has meant that we believe we are now on the verge of obtaining an anti-dote".

"On the verge – but not quite there yet?" said Kenneth in interrogative tone.

"Exactly. And this is where you come in."

"I'm a physicist, not a medical practitioner or bio-chemist".

"We know. However, as I'm sure you'll understand, we can't simply administer the anti-dote in the conventional way by setting up vaccination centres around the world", laughed Von Hildeger."

"Well eh no", said Kenneth with a wry grin.

"We had thought of sending the anti-dote substance into the Earth's atmosphere in canisters and releasing them into the stratosphere but there are innumerable technical and logistical problems in that method about which I won't go into detail right now."

"I can see what they are", said Kenneth. "You would need to ensure it would reach ground level without being destroyed before it got there. You would also need to ensure against it being mal-distributed by winds. How could you be sure it got to the right people?"

"Exactly. But there's more. Even if it worked, the Nazis would simply apply their own drugs again. Almost all of the world's military and police personnel are under their control now through their PC stooges. So even without the Nazi drug, the liberated minds would be unable to do anything about it. Likewise, we here on Mars can do nothing about it as we do not have the man-power for military confrontation."

"So what then is the point of this anti-dote? It all looks like an exercise in futility to me."

"Have you heard of the asteroid Apophis?"

"Yes. It quite often has come dangerously close to the Earth."

"Kenneth. Next year it will strike the Earth."

"What?"

"There is nothing that can be done about it. It is due to land in the Arizona desert next year."

"That will throw reflective dust particles up into the air and bring on another ice age in around ten years."

"Yes, but there is an upside to this. It will kill off the Nazis. Their underground facilities are not a quarter as advanced as our ones on Mars. They will freeze to death".

"But so will a lot of innocent people – like my parents and Hilary".

"Apophis is a reality Kenneth and there is nothing we can do about it. However, we can minimise the effects".

"How?"

"First of all, in conjunction with our rocket scientists and engineers, we want you to devise a system whereby Apophis takes the anti-dote to Earth. This way the asteroid can be a means of deliverance as well as of death and destruction."

"And how do you see this being accomplished?"

"We have been making regular trips to Apophis in our spacecrafts. There, we have been storing large supplies of the anti-dote. We have enough to cover the entire Earth about three times over. But, and this is the big but, we need to develop some sort of rocket system which fires off the anti-dote equally in all directions and just at the point when Apophis is in the lower stratosphere and just above the troposphere."

"And then?"

"When minds are eventually liberated from the poison of political correctness, we will announce the Apophis strike and the coming ice age."

"And what next?"

"Our calculations show that the strike will be sufficient to blot out the sun in the northern hemisphere only".

"What are your calculations based upon?"

"The size of the asteroid and the force of its impact."

"Also, innocent people need not die. Those whose minds remain unaffected by the PC drugs will do the common sense thing and move southwards to equatorial and southern hemispherical regions. Those who are so convinced about global warming will remain and freeze. Good riddance to them."

"But don't the Nazis have heating and life support systems in their underground caverns?"

"No. We are ahead of them because from the outset we have had to devise our life support technology on a cold planet."

"Now, another question. How do you know the anti-dote will work? Have you been able to do tests?"

"Not yet."

"Well how can you be so sure about its efficacy?"

"Tomorrow you will see. First let me drop you off at your new home. Get a good night's sleep, and tomorrow we shall commence work."

The car drove up to a very large three storey villa. It was one of the most magnificent houses Kenneth had ever seen. It was surrounded on all four sides with lawns and with gardens that had all manner of exotic looking trees and plants growing in them.

"This is some size of a house", said Kenneth.

"Well, you'll be sharing it with two others", replied Von Hildeger.

"Even so. It is quite a size".

Kenneth and Von Hildeger alighted from the car and walked along the graveled pathway to the main door. Von Hildeger rang the bell. When the door was opened, Kenneth almost died of astonishment. There to greet him were William and Morag Mackenzie. They were just as astonished to see their son. The three of them ran towards each other in a fond embrace of weeping.

"I wanted this to be a surprise for all of you", said Von Hildeger.

"It's a wonderful surprise", said William.

"You'll have a lot to talk about, so I'll take my leave".

"Won't you stay for some refreshment Dr. Von Hildeger?" Morag asked.

"Thank you Mrs. Mackenzie but I really must get going".

The family, united again, recounted their experiences since the day of that awful court case in former Scotland. As had been the case with Kenneth, his parents also had been clandestinely spirited away by the 'Martians' for their own protection against the vengeful apparatchiks of Political Correctness.

"What happened to you in both the court and in Bruce's cave Kenneth, shows that Almighty God has a mission for you", said Morag.

"Political Correctness is truly a Godless evil", William added.

The following morning Von Hildeger collected Kenneth from his home. They drove to the main research station in Radiant City. On the way there Kenneth expressed his thanks to Von Hildeger for his kindness in looking after his parents, but there was something else he wanted to know.

"You've been very kind Dr. Von Hildeger, but have you any idea about my fiancé Hilary Jennings?"

"I'll explain everything about Hilary a little later", replied Von Hildeger rather solemnly.

Kenneth became a little startled: "Is she… is she….?"

"She's all right Kenneth, she's all right, but please be patient".

The two men walked across the car park to the main building in silence. They walked through a maze of corridors until they finally stopped at a room marked 'sanatorium'. Kenneth's heart began to pound wildly. Inside, he saw three people sitting around a table and eating. They looked at Kenneth and Von Hildeger, and they looked back at them. Kenneth heart leapt for joy when he saw his fiancé Hilary and his two friends Roger Edmore and Patricia Towler. Kenneth rushed towards Hilary with outstretched arms.

"Hilary darling, I'm so happy to see you. Oh my love, I've been so worried about you."

"Keep away from me you racist, Nazi pig. You fascist piece of filth, don't come near me".

"Hilary! Why?", said Kenneth, the tears welling up in his eyes.

"Leave her alone, you politically incorrect piece of garbage", said Roger.

"You gang of kidnappers. You bigoted scum."

"You were taken to Mars for your own good" explained Kenneth.

"Mars!" shrieked Patricia, throwing her head back and letting out an hysterical laugh. "How can we be on Mars. Mars is only a small dot of light in the sky. How could this be Mars?"

Hilary, Patricia and Roger then started to bang their fists on the table and to chant slogans such as 'fascist bastards', 'racist pigs', 'Nazi scum'. Three nurses and three orderlies walked into the room and physically restrained the three of them. The nurses applied the nozzles of gas cylinders to the three patients who were then led off to their beds in a comatose condition.

"I know that Hilary was attacked and drugged", said Kenneth, "but she was all right the last time I saw her on Earth".

"It was a delayed reaction, Kenneth. I'm sorry to show you all this but you must face reality. However, there is hope for your fiancé and two friends. The anti-dote is ready for trials and these three will be the first recipients."

"But you're using them as guinea pigs", protested Kenneth.

"Oh Kenneth. What else can we do? We have to begin somewhere", replied Von Hildeger somewhat impatiently.

"It is an untested and unproven serum. Who knows, it may kill them."

"I'm sorry Kenneth", said Von Hildeger sympathetically but firmly, "it is a chance we just have to take".

"Well, all right", said Kenneth rather reluctantly.

"Now, I want you to meet our chief medical officer, Professor Stephen Latimore. He is in his office waiting for us."

CHAPTER 12.
YOU!!

There was another shock in store for Kenneth when he walked into Professor Stephen Latimore's office.

"Dr. Von Hildeger", said Kenneth with hate and anger in his voice, "this man is an imposter. He is a spy. This is no Professor Stephen Latimore, this is Angus Davidson, the green cheese moon man".

"Calm down Kenneth, calm down. He is a spy and he is an imposter but on our side. He was born and bred on Mars and came to Earth as a spy six years ago."

"Kenneth, I'm sorry if I startled you", said Latimore. "I came to Earth to spy on the PC system which is overpowering your planet."

"Not only that, but Stephen managed to collect the blood samples from drugged patients which we so desperately needed. Before Stephen went to Earth all our research for an anti-dote was theoretically based. Thanks to both his bravery and intelligence, our research has advanced in leaps and bounds. We did in five years what had eluded us for around 80 years."

"And what about all this green cheese nonsense?" asked Kenneth.

"I had to see how far the lunacy had gone."

Von Hildeger then informed Stephen about Kenneth's concerns about the vaccine.

"Kenneth, I hold doctorates in medicine and bio-chemistry", said Stephen.

"Well, Stephen, that doesn't make you infallible", replied Kenneth. "However, I have agreed that the anti-dote be applied".

"When shall we administer the anti-dote?" Von Hildeger asked.

"In one hour, when the patients are recovering from the sedative gas", Stephen replied.

When Kenneth, Von Hildeger and Stephen went into the room where Hilary, Roger and Patricia lay, Kenneth asked if they were ready now to be injected.

"This anti-dote will be given in gaseous form. The room will be sprayed with the gas anti-dote. This is how it will be applied on a wide scale on Earth", Stephen explained.

Stephen then asked Kenneth and Von Hildeger to get into pressure suits and oxygen masks. When the three were thus clad, Stephen Latimore started spraying. Two minutes later he directed his two colleagues to leave the room. He then closed the door behind Hilary, Roger and Patricia.

"All we can do now is wait", Stephen explained.

"For how long?" Kenneth asked.

"I want to give it an hour", said Stephen. He then pointed to a monitor where he could view the patients. "This contraption here", he said while walking over to another monitor, will measure the level of gas in the room. When it is low enough, we shall enter."

Half an hour later, the three patients began to stir; first Roger, then Hilary and lastly Patricia.

"Where are we?" Hilary asked

"I don't know", Roger answered.

"It looks like a private room in a hospital of some kind", commented Patricia.

"But, but, I don't understand. How did we get here. I can't remember coming here", said Patricia.

"Did we have an accident and lose consciousness, I wonder?" said Roger.

"This is very strange", said Hilary. Hilary got up and started walking around the room. "I'll try and find a window", she said. "Strange, no windows".

"It looks like the anti-dote is a success", said Kenneth as he watched the monitor with Von Hildeger and Stephen.

"Yes", said Stephen, "but they will need to be closely monitored for some time in case of relapse".

"Can I go in and speak to Hilary now?", asked Kenneth desperately.

Stephen looked at the gas gauge: "Wait – levels of the gas are still too high".

An hour later it was considered safe to enter.

"Hilary!" exclaimed Kenneth.

"Kenneth! Oh Kenneth. Where have you been?"

They hugged each other in fond embrace.

"What's going on here Kenneth?" Roger asked.

"Where are we?" asked Patricia.

For the next hour, Kenneth, Stephen and Von Hildeger explained everything.

"Oh Kenneth", said Hilary with downcast eyes. "To think that I called you all those nasty names. I am so sorry. I am so ashamed of myself. In fact, I'm disgusted with myself".

"Don't apologise", Kenneth told her. "You were under the spell of an evil narcotic".

"It was not your fault", Von Hildeger explained.

"We would like you to stay in hospital here for a few more days so that we can monitor your progress", Stephen told his three patients.

"Then we'll take you to your accommodation", Von Hildeger informed them.

When they left the three patients to recuperate, Von Hildeger turned to Stephen and said, "well, young man, it looks like your anti-dote works".

"Yes", replied Stephen. "I just hope that the culprit drug is completely out of their systems. We'll know soon enough once we do blood tests."

"I have another question", said Kenneth. "How do we inform the Earth about the Apophis strike?"

"We are still working on that. There is about one year remaining before the strike, so we must get moving on a delivery system for the anti-dote. The robots which we have landed on Apophis are being directed from Mars. They are conveying the anti-dote to various parts of the 1,100 foot asteroid."

"How exactly is this done?"

Rudolph Von Hildeger led Kenneth into a large laboratory.

"Kenneth. This is Dr. Wilhelm Schneiderer, the controller of our rocket research project"

"I look forward to working with you doctor", said Kenneth.

"Kenneth was wondering exactly how we direct our robots on Apophis", said Von Hildeger.

"We walk on Apophis", said Schneiderer smiling.

"You mean you send manned missions there?" Kenneth asked.

"Initially yes", replied Schneiderer, "but robotic systems have taken over now".

"I don't then understand what you mean by 'walking on Apophis'", said Kenneth with a puzzled look on his face.

"Come into this cubicle", said Schneiderer.

The three of them walked towards a contraption that looked like the Tardis from Dr. Who. Once inside, Schneiderer pressed a button and all at once the three men were standing on Apophis.

"This is a three dimensional film of Apophis", Schneiderer explained. The entire asteroid is covered with cameras. You can walk around the asteroid. Face any direction you like and just lift your feet up and down. The cameras will read the speed and direction of your footsteps and bring into detail the particular parts of the asteroid you are walking on".

The three men 'walked' all over the asteroid and saw the various pieces of robotic equipment that the Mars community had landed there. Wilhelm Schneiderer showed Kenneth the large stock piles of anti-dote which had been brought there over the past two years by manned and robotic missions.

"And can you activate and direct the robots here?" Kenneth asked.

"Yes indeed", Schneiderer replied. "It's just like actually being there".

"And another thing", added Von Hildeger, "we shall be on this asteroid when it discharges the anti-dote and when it crashes on to the Earth – in this booth of course", he added reassuringly.

CHAPTER 13.
Courting Trouble.

One year later, Kenneth and Shneiderer had succeeded in developing a means by which the anti-dote on Apophis could be discharged over the Earth. Things were certainly looking up on all fronts as Hilary, Roger and Patricia showed no signs of relapse. Their blood samples had shown that the Nazi narcotic was completely eliminated by Stephen Latimore's anti-dote.

Everything went according to plan. Hundreds of canisters of gaseous anti-dote were released over the Earth just before the asteroid crashed into the Arizona Desert. Inside the 'Tardis' there was an almighty explosion and everything went blank when all the electronic equipment on the asteroid was destroyed on impact.

Kenneth, Von Hildeger and Schneiderer were sitting in Von Hildeger's office considering the next move.

"Here is the answer to the question you posed last year Kenneth regarding how we alert the Earth people to the catastrophe."

Judge John Benson reconvened the Great Court of Political Correctness in Europe's Mid- Region 12.

"Bring on the Guilty", hollered Benson.

An old man of about 75 was brought into the dock.

"Citizen 345BV23, you have been spreading malicious gossip about the Apophis strike and how it will cause an ice age in about ten years time".

"I'm not spreading rumours", protested the man. "Everyone is talking about it."

"And precisely how did you come by this information?"

"I heard it on the radio".

"Which station?"

"I don't know. I only came across it by accident. It broadcast once and then went off the air. I've never been able to pick it up again".

"Ahahh", cried Benson, "you have been tuning into the pirate radio stations of politically incorrect dissidents. You know what a serious offence that is."

"I didn't 'tune in'", the elderly man said, "this message – it, it, it em it just came on!"

"All right – thank you for the moment. Call in Professor Donald Morrison."

"Professor Morrison, what is your take on all of this?"

"Well, it has been confirmed that something large from outer space landed in the Arizona Desert in the USA. Many scientists are saying that the dust particles thrown up will eventually result in the sunlight being blocked out. The long and the short of it is that there will be another ice age."

"But are these scientists politically correct?"

"Well, I'm not too sure about that. I would guess not because what they are predicting goes against the whole concept of global warming."

"Now! About these reflective dust particles. What can be done to eliminate them so that they do not interfere with the theories regarding global warming?"

"This is a tricky one. With respect to you Your Political Correctness, but global warming is not a theory, it is a proven and incontrovertible fact."

"Then what can we do to stop these particles getting in the way of our incontrovertible facts?"

"I'd need some time to think about it, Your Political Correctness".

Later that day, Donald Morrison's secretary announced a visitor. "This is Professor Dr. Gustaf Krobels".

"Good afternoon Professor Morrison. I was in court today and I think I can help you out of your predicament with regard to those dust particles".

"First of all, Professor Dr. Krobels, may I see your credentials?"

Krobels then proceeded to hand over some documentation to Morrison.

"I see", said Morrison becoming more relaxed and looking pleased, "that you are from the elite Institute of Political Correctness in Berlin. Most impressive, Herr Professor Doctor. And what exactly is your proposal regarding dealing with the dust particles?"

"It is this", said Krobels, and then proceeded to explain it in detail to Morrison.

"That's an excellent idea", commented Morrison. "Would you be so kind, Professor Doctor as to come to tomorrow's court session?"

The following day, Morrison and Krobels went to the Great Court of Political Correctness to explain to Judge Benson Krobels' idea for dealing with the dust particles.

"It's absolutely brilliant", said Benson. "Let's get it off to Brussels through the European Representative for Political Correctness for Mid-Region 12 immediately".

A few days later legislation was rushed through the European Parliament. The law enacted that: "the dust particles are totally forbidden by the great and glorious laws of the nation of Europe to block out the sun. Furthermore, anyone who states that the dust particles will prevent sunlight reaching the Earth and/or anyone who says that they will be the causative agent of another ice age, will be deemed guilty of the most heinous, horrific and abominable offence and will so be put on trial under the European laws of blasphemy, high treason and treachery. Anyone who is found guilty of encouraging the dust particles to block out the sun, will be sent to a labour camp for the rest of their lives."

At Radiant City on Mars, Schneiderer, Von Hildeger and Latimore, explained to Kenneth Mackenzie a method that the scientists on Mars had developed to ensure that the dust particles would not cause another ice age.

"There are four of our VTFCs flying in formation over the Earth's northern hemisphere. They are scouring the stratosphere with laser beams which are being shone out from the craft. These laser beams are forcing the dust particles downwards to ground level. Within about one month at the most, the stratosphere should be cleared of dust particles", Von Hildeger explained.

"Why didn't you tell me all this before?" Kenneth asked.

"We can never be too cautious when it comes to security".

"All right, I understand", replied Kenneth somewhat grumpily.

"It's not that we don't trust you Kenneth", said Stephen Latimore. "You might talk in your sleep, or it may just slip".

"Anyway", came in Shneiderer, "we want to tell you now something even more important. It is how we are going to once and for all defeat the Nazis and, in all practical terms, end World War II".

Back on Earth, it was a mixture of good news and bad news for the President of Europe. Chairing a session of the Supreme Council of Europe, the President and his ministers listened attentively to the latest reports from the European Regions and from elsewhere around the world.

"I suppose I'll start with the bad news", said the President.

The Minister of Thought Control obsequiously cleared his throat and proceeded thus: "something very strange is happening. Peoples' minds are being enslaved in political incorrectness. They are rejecting the great enlightenment of the politically correct renaissance and adopting ideas which go...."

The President banged his fist on the table and yelled "oh cut the bloody crap would you? Tell me what the hell is going on".

The Minister of Thought Control started to look very thoughtful and more obsequious than ever. "In eh eh in simple terms...", at this point the Minister took a deep breath and continued in mournful tones, "the effects of the drug are wearing off."

"Is the effect wearing off or is it being caused by an anti-dote?"

"We don't know yet. We will have to investigate this matter a lot further before we really know."

"And the good news?"

The Minister of Political Correctness shuffled his papers and told the President and Council that many places in the northern hemisphere were covered in fine dust particles. As the sun had not been blotted out, he said that it would be reasonable to conclude that the dust particles had fallen faster than expected.

"Why have they fallen so fast?" the President asked.

"It seems that the legislation we enacted recently has had the desired effect", said the Minister.

The President, with his right fist under his chin, his elbow on the table and an exasperated look on his face, said to the Minister of PC, " puleeze, puleeze, keep all that for the propaganda announcements. In the meantime, don't insult my intelligence."

CHAPTER 14.
Worlds War II.

"So, apart from the four spacecraft in the stratosphere, what else is there?" Mackenzie asked Von Hildeger.

"We have seven more craft at higher orbit waiting for orders from the Military High Command here on Mars."

"Now this is where Phase 1 of the operation comes into play", said Latimore

"What exactly is it?" Kenneth asked.

Von Hildeger, Latimore and Shneiderer proceeded to explain this first phase of Operation Nazi Clear-out.

"Where the hell is Mulinger?" asked an angry President of Europe to his Chief of Narcotics Supply.

"We seem to have lost all contact with him", replied the Chief.

"Well, it could be taking a bit longer as we need so many times more the usual supply from Pedro Gonzages".

As usual, Mulinger's VTFC landed near Gonzages' private airstrip. The aircraft took off after having deposited Mulinger on the ground with his six armed body guards. As always, they would wait for Gonzages to arrive in person to collect his most valued customer.

This had been the procedure for the past 100 years, so the descendants of the original Gonzages and the descendants of the original Mulinger had no reason to think that it would be any different now. However something that was a tad different did happen. Mulinger and his body guards heard a strange buzzing sound in the sky. They looked up and saw a massive VTFC; it must have been at least 30 times the size of their one. This new VTFC fired a missile at the puny little VTFC in which Mulinger had flown in and blew it out of existence. Mulinger and his body guards were stunned into speechlessness. They just stared up at the sky hardly believing their eyes and ears.

Suddenly, there was a burst of fire. Mulinger's six body guards bit the dust. Mulinger was petrified. He looked around in all directions but could see no-one. He whipped out his mobile 'phone, but before he could contact anyone, twenty commandoes jumped out of the bushes nearby and surrounded the terrified man.

"Who are you?" asked a shaking and quaking Mulinger.

"Ve vill ask zi questionz", said their leader mockingly.

The commandoes motioned Mulinger into the thick growth at the side of the air-strip.

When Gonzages and his body guards arrived on the scene, they got out of their car and looked around in bewilderment. They saw the corpses of the body guards but nothing of Mulinger. There was a sudden burst of automatic fire and Gonzages and his body guards crumpled up and fell to the ground.

"Now", said the commander of the commandoes, "radio your plane to come. And by the way, I speak fluent German, so no funny stuff."

Mulinger reluctantly did as he was told. A few minutes later the plane could be seen approaching. The Martian VTFC descended from above and shot the plane out of the air. The VTFC then landed in a poppy field near the air-strip. Mulinger was ordered inside. He was absolutely astonished at the technological sophistication he witnessed. The VTFC then started to ascend.

"Look at this screen", said Tony Kent.

Mulinger did so. To his horror he saw the bungalow, factories, storehouses, truck depots and all the infra-structure of the narcotics plantation being bombed to match-sticks. Next, the VTFC sprayed the thousands of acres with a chemical.

"This will ensure", said Kent looking hard at Mulinger, "that these fields will never grow narcotics again."

Mulinger was now trembling with fear. "Who are you and what do you want with me? I have a right to know."

"We need some information from you Herr Mulinger – and we need it fast. First of all tell us the exact locations of the entrances to the underground Nazi network."

Mulinger looked at his captor in amazement. "How do you know about that? Who sent you…who are you?" said Mulinger beside himself with rage.

"We don't have a second of time to waste Mulinger", said Kent taking out a revolver and pointing it at Mulinger's head.

"If I tell you, you'll kill me anyway. So I don't have to tell you anything."

Kent nodded to a nurse and two soldiers who came over to where Kent and Mulinger were standing. The soldier pulled up his shirt sleeve and the nurse administered an injection."

Kent walked away from Mulinger and spoke to the commander of the squad. "Give the truth drug a bit of time to take hold and we'll question him again".

Mulinger became slightly drowsy as the drug began to kick in.

"Now", said Kent, "let's start again. Where are the entrances to the tunnels located?"

Mulinger told Kent that there were 50 of them dotted around Europe and North America.

"Do you have any other narcotics suppliers - apart than Gonzages".

"None", replied the doped Mulinger.

"And how far do the underground networks extend?" said Kent continuing his interrogation.

"They extend far – right into ministries, universities, private homes and a host of other establishments".

"What is their life support system?"

"The entrances are located in either disused mines or fake mining operations. Some are located in remote mountainous regions. The main control rooms are located in large complexes near the shafts. This room provides ventilation and air. It also provides the electrical power for the area network of tunnels".

"And what would happen if these were destroyed by missiles?"

"Everyone below would suffocate in a fairly short time."

"The next question. Who are the real Nazis who are working above ground? What positions do they hold and where can your leaders be found?"

The Governing Council on Mars was a body made up of the citizens of the various underground cities of the red planet. There were no full-time politicians on Mars and bureaucracy was kept to a minimum. All citizens over the age of 25 were expected to serve on the 30 man Council. The Governing Council met in the large Mars Council Building in the capital, Cydonia City. The massive underground 25 mile diameter complex made Kenneth wonder whether or not he had somehow been mysteriously transported back to Earth.

"Would the Chief of Military Operations please apprise the Council as to what has been conveyed from the squadrons operating on Earth?" the Chairman of the Council asked.

"Yes Mr. Chairman. We have now the exact locations of all the underground tunnels the Nazis are using on Earth. We also have the names of all the Nazi leaders clandestinely working above ground." The Chief then proceeded to read out the names. "Furthermore, we have killed Gonzages and laid waste his narcotics fields – so there will be no more drug supplies to the Nazis."

"Mr. Mackenzie. I believe you have a suggestion for Phase 2 of the operation".

Kenneth stood up and told the council what he thought should be the next phase of the operation.

Kent's VTFC hovered above a disused coal mine in the West Midlands of England. Kent ordered the medical staff to give Mulinger another shot of truth drug. This drug had been developed by the scientists of Mars. It was developed mainly to stamp out crime. It blocked oxygen supplies to the areas of the brain which dealt with imaginary and creative thought processes. When these were temporarily shut down, it was therefore impossible for any suspect on Mars to tell anything other than the truth without being very quickly found out. The reason this pharmaceutical had been given such high priority was because of the limited resources on Mars, and the great urgency with which the new 'Martians' would have to proceed in their immediate need for survival. They simply could not afford to waste valuable time and resources on social work and police activities. Now this drug was being put to a use far beyond its original purpose.

"Now Herr Mulinger", said Kent pointing at the monitor, "is that the control room".

"Yes", replied Mulinger.

"Captain", said Kent. "Prepare to fire missiles at the control room.

"Yes sir", replied the captain.

Everything went completely dark all of a sudden in the Nazi underground complex which controlled the West Midlands tunnels. Contact was attempted with the surface control room, but to no avail. Very soon the oxygen was running low and everyone scrambled for the lifts, but there was no power to operate them. They were doomed to suffocate in their underground bunkers.

The same operation was performed for the remaining 49 control rooms. Under the influence of the truth drug, Mulinger pointed out all the installations that would have to be destroyed in order to make the underground networks inoperative. Phase 2 was declared to be a success.

Before returning to Mars, the VTFCs dropped more canisters of the anti-dote over the Earth. Minds started awakening as if from a Rip Van Winkle type sleep. Their memories were sometimes vague regarding the politically correct years, but they remembered enough to know that a terrible con had been pulled on them. All over Western Europe and north America, civil war broke out between the politically correct and the politically incorrect. There simply had not been sufficient anti-dote to reach everyone. However, the politically correct were always a small elite. So it was not long before the hitherto silent, cowed, brow-beaten – not to mention drugged and mind-altered – people overcame their politically correct Nazi masters and overlords. Bloody civil war raged throughout Europe and North America for a whole year. With minds open to reason and common sense and with the underground Nazis dead, there was little that the successors of Hitler operating above ground could do.

The War Cabinet on Mars met to consider Phase 3 of Operation Nazi Clear Out. The War Cabinet was a small group of people which consisted of Kenneth Mackenzie, Dr. Rudolph Von Hildeger, Dr. Wilhelm Shneiderer, Dr. Stephen Latimore and the Chief of Military Operations.

"What is the location of the VTFCs now?" asked Kenneth.

"They are approaching Earth's moon and should be in Earth orbit in two days", replied the Chief.

"Most of the politically correct forces have surrendered and only small pockets of resistance remain. Those who have been captured will soon be given the anti-dote to clear their minds".

"Could we make this a major priority?" the military chief asked. "Our contacts on Earth inform us that the prison camps are overcrowded and the scarcity of food caused by hostilities makes it increasingly difficult to feed the growing number of prisoners".

"We understand", said Von Hildeger. "Please issue instructions to your VTFC commanders to make the distribution of the anti-dote the first priority".

"Kenneth", said Wilhelm Schneiderer, "you have studied the list of above-ground Nazi operatives. Could you please draw up a plan for the destruction of the buildings and facilities from which they operate?"

"Yes", replied Kenneth. "After this meeting has ended, I shall sit down with the Chief of Military Operations and work out a detailed plan for the elimination of Nazi operative centres masquerading as politically correct institutions. However, as in line with Cabinet's policy, this Phase will be effected once the anti-dote has been successfully distributed."

On board the VTFC flagship, the Captain approached Tony Kent with a list. He saluted Kent and said "This is a list of all the prisoner of war camps on Earth. There are one hundred of them dotted around Western Europe and North America. As you will see sir, next to each camp is the anti-dote, the amount being as calculated by the various camp governors."

"Do we have sufficient supplies with us to meet all the requirements?" Kent asked.

"Provisionally we can say that we do. However, in actual practice, we cannot be certain. Only time alone will tell".

"The War Cabinet wants these distributed as quickly as possible so that we can, without any further delay, enact Phase 3 of Operation Nazi Clear Out".

Each of the ten VTFCs were allotted ten camps to which they were to distribute the anti-dote. Within two days the anti-dote was distributed around the world. Phase 3 was now to be implemented.

CHAPTER 15.
The Devil Looks After His Own - Usually.

"This President of Europe", said Tony Kent to the Chief of Narcotics Supplies who had been captured by the Resistance, "tell us exactly who he is".

Under the influence of the truth drug, the peddler in death told Kent, "his name is not Monsieur Pierre du Nouard, his real name is Adolph Hitler. He is the great, great, great grandson of the first Adolph Hitler."

"And where can we find him now?"

"Most likely in the underground bunker near the presidential palace in Brussels."

When the narcotics man had given the exact location of the bunker, Kent informed the Resistance field commanders in Brussels.

The game was up for Adolph Hitler. The European Parliament buildings in Luxembourg and Strasbourg were smoldering ashes. Not a stone upon stone remained of the United Nations building in New York. The so-called 'Scottish Parliament' was ablaze as were the Welsh and English Regional Assembly meeting places. The Allies were only a few miles from Hitler's Brussels bunker and the sound of approaching Resistance vehicles could be clearly heard. Their deafening noise told Hitler that it was all over. The great great great grandson of Martin Bormann advised the great great great grandson of Adolph Hitler that further delay would result in capture. Adolph Hitler nodded in agreement.

"Is the plan ready to be put into operation?", asked the Fuhrer.

"All the details have been meticulously worked out and the first step in its implementation should be taken as soon as possible Mein Fuhrer", Bormann replied.

Bormann left the room and went into his own office. He strolled over to his desk and opened one of the drawers. He slowly but confidently took out a revolver; he put just one bullet into it. He then walked out of the room with the revolver.

In the Fuhrer's living quarters in the bunker, Bormann walked over to the little, bald, clean shaven man and asked him to look closely at the revolver. The little, bald, clean shaven man did so and Bormann pulled the trigger and blew his head clean away. Bormann then walked through to the main operations room of the bunker.

"Step one of the plan has been completed", said Bormann.

A, bearded man with a full head of hair who was sitting facing the wall quickly swiveled round and simply stared at Bormann.

"Which look-alike did you use?" the man asked Bormann.

"Number 3. He was the best of the six impersonators."

"Excellent, excellent", replied the hairy man.

"Mein Fuhrer", said Bormann rather nervously, "we must now, with the utmost haste, implement step 2 of the Great Plan".

"Yes yes", replied the totally be-wigged and bearded Fuhrer.

Hitler and Bormann walked over to a portion of the office wall. Bormann removed a painting from the wall and laid it carefully on a chair nearby. The painting's removal revealed a single, solitary button. Bormann pressed this button and, as if by magic, two parts of the wall, each about four feet across and eight feet high, parted to reveal a lift. Hitler stepped into the lift and Bormann followed. The doors closed and Hitler and Bormann descended two hundred feet underground. In the main operations room, one of Bormann's minions unscrewed the button and deactivated the lift's mechanism. The wall looked like a wall again, and the doors were sealed forever. The picture was replaced to where it had previously been.

Two hundred feet underground, a long train was waiting for Hitler and Bormann. A staff officer standing erect motioned Hitler and Bormann to one of the compartments.

Once seated in the train compartment, an officer with the rank of colonel came up to Hitler and Bormann. He clicked his heels and gave the Nazi salute.

"Are all 500 of our handpicked Nazi patriots safely ensconced on this train, Colonel Rontler", inquired the Fuhrer.

"They are Mein Fuhrer", replied Colonel Rontler.

"Good. Then let us delay no longer".

Colonel Rontler stepped out of the compartment and motioned to a man who was standing on the platform. The man raised a small flag which he was holding in his hand. In his other hand he held a whistle. He applied the whistle to his lips and soon the train started to move off.

"I'm so disappointed the Fuhrer managed to commit suicide", said Kenneth to his mother, father and Hilary. "I really wanted to get my hands on that bastard".

"You know something Kenneth", said William Mackenzie thoughtfully and seriously, "your mother and I were talking about that just a little while ago".

"Your father and I are not scientists but we are political analysts", said Morag Mackenzie.

"Weren't you both lecturers in Political Science at Edinburgh University?" Hilary asked.

"Yes we were", answered Morag.

"Kenneth", continued William, "our studies show that politics tends to go round in circles. A sort of 'what goes around comes around'. Things often appear to be mirror images of each other, but although the mirror shows left and right as opposites, although script appears to be in reverse, it is still the same image and the message of the script is still the same. The image reverses but the substance remains exactly the same. Nazism and Political Correctness may be opposites in image appearance, but their essence and substance are exactly the same."

"We are sure that the corpse they found in the bunker in Brussels is not that of the President of Europe – the Fuhrer, in other words", said Morag. "As Hitler used a substitute back in 1945 so the descendant has done exactly the same. You see the substance remains unchanged."

"Where the image reversal comes into play", said William, "is in the appearance. The 20th century Hitler shaved off his moustache and hair. So the bald and beardless 21st century Hitler will be disguised as a bearded man with a full head of hair".

"But where did the real Hitler go – I mean the current one?" asked Hilary.

Everyone thought for a moment.

"If the original Hitler escaped by means of an underground rail network, then the present one did the same. This is where your theory of political imagery and rotation come into play", reasoned Hilary.

"Good thinking Hilary", commented Morag.

"But where did our present day Hitler go?"

"To solve that one", said William, "let's ask where the original Hitler went".

"We really don't know", said Kenneth shaking his head.

"But we can use a bit of reasoning power", said William. "Where is the nearest politically correct establishment to Berlin?"

"That would be Strasbourg", said Morag.

"Yes, it's around 366 miles from Berlin", William confirmed.

"Was it within the first third of the 20th century's technological ability to construct an underground rail network between Berlin and Strasbourg?" Hilary asked.

"You're the scientist Ken", said William gesturing to his son.

"Yes, I think it would have been".

"Then, I would make the reasoned conjecture that Hitler ended his train journey in Strasbourg and alighted more or less in the vicinity of the EU parliament building there", explained William.

Kenneth jumped up with great excitement. "We can't waste any more time. Let me contact Tony Kent right away".

"Well Kenneth", said Tony Kent who was now at Army High Command HQ in Brussels and was communicating by radio between Earth and Mars, "I see your reasoning, but I fear it may be too late."

"It depends upon the speed of the train. And they'll have preparatory work to do in the way of getting everyone on board and ensuring various supplies are loaded onto the carriages."

"All right", I'll get a military detachment there immediately.

Inside Adolph Hitler's bunker in Berlin, a man removed a painting from a wall in what had been Hitler's office. At the other side of the wall, Martin Bormann the Fifth pressed a button and the walls separated. Martin Bormann entered the 100 year old bunker. It took around two hours to get all the passengers up to ground level. Last to arrive was Adolph Hitler the Fifth. The painting was replaced on the wall.

"Is the coast clear?" Hitler asked Bormann.

"Yes Mein Fuhrer", answered the loyal henchman.".

"Ahhh", rasped Hitler, "all this worked for our forebears, it will work for us too".

"Now without further delay Mein Fuhrer", cautioned Bormann, "we must work while it is still dark and get our supplies unloaded from the train."

By early morning, all the supplies had been off-loaded

"Let us now assemble outside in the courtyard", said Hitler.

Dawn was breaking on a lovely summer's morning over Berlin. Hitler stood in front of the loyal 500 and told them he would inform them of the next phase of the operation. Before he could do that a hundred heavily armed soldiers surrounded the fugitives and instructed them to put their hands in the air. Some tried to run for it but warning shots fired into the air forced them back. They were trapped. There was no escape.

Tony Kent approached Hitler. "Good morning Mein Fuhrer", he said sneeringly.

"I...I... don't know what you're talking about", answered Hitler.

Kent pulled the wig from Hitler's head. The Fuhrer was then shaven on the spot. There was Adolph Hitler alias Monsieur Pierre du Nouard, the President of Europe.

CHAPTER 16.
Mea Culpa, Mea Culpa, Mea Maxima Culpa.

Adolph Hitler, under the truth drug, made a full confession on television to the entire world. He was interviewed on the re-constituted BBC, a BBC now shorn of its political correctness. The interviewer began by asking Hitler about what his plans had been for the world.

Int: It is significant that you were captured on May 8th 2045 – exactly 100 years after V E Day.

Hit: Yes I suppose it is.

Int: The Second World War is now truly over. You have been defeated militarily – twice, and though you were on the verge of winning through subterfuge in political methods and narcotic substances, you were eventually defeated in these arenas too. Do you know how you were found out and how you were defeated?

Hit: Either the effects of the drug wore off or some kind of anti-dote was manufactured – I don't know. We could never work out how.

Int: Well it was by the widespread use of an anti-dote.

Hit: How did you discover our underground network?

Int: Ve vill ask zi questionz Herr Fuhrer. (laughs from the audience)

The interviewer explained to the audience and to viewers all about the colonies on Mars and about the adventures of Kenneth Mackenzie.

Int: Now Mr. Hitler. What exactly was your intention had you succeeded in your evil plans?

Hit: It was to set up the Fourth Reich.

Int: Wouldn't this have caused some confusion among the politically correct who were convinced that PCism was anti-Nazi?

Hit: Their minds were so confused anyway because of the narcotics we pumped into them. They would have swallowed anything.

Int: And precisely what was it they were supposed to swallow?

Hit: That Nazism and Political Correctness were brotherly philosophies.

Int: That would have been the only truth you and your ilk would ever have told.

Hit: Yes.

Int: Why did the latter-day Nazis wish to flood Western Europe and North America with third world and East European immigrants?

Hit: We were defeated in two world wars. We wanted revenge. This was our way of getting back at the allies. It was our intention to undermine western culture, religion and political institutions. We wanted all those who had died protecting the British way of life to have died in vain.

Int: You are the great great great grandson of the first Adolph Hitler. Tell us about your lineage.

Hit: The first Adolph Hitler had a secret son by Eva Braun. All the direct male descendants of the first Adolph Hitler were named Adolph.

Int: Your son and grandson have been taken into custody. Your grandson will be brought up as a good anti-Nazi, a *genuine* anti-Nazi as he is still only five years of age.

Hit: And my son and I?

Int: You will no doubt be tried and if found guilty, as you most assuredly will be, then you and your son will be executed. Ah we have a question from the audience.

BG: My name is Barry Gordon. Can we be sure that this man is really the Fuhrer? What about the corpse found in the Brussels bunker?

Int: The truth drug that this man before you is now under and the DNA testing performed on both him and the corpse proves beyond all reasonable doubt that this is Adolph Hitler masquerading as Pierre du Nouard. Ah another question from the audience. The lady in the blue dress in the back row.

AA: My name is Alison Ackland. Where will the trials take place?

Int: In Nuremburg I would think.

CHAPTER 17.
The New Jerusalem.

Three months later Kenneth returned to his home town of Annan to receive a hero's welcome. There to greet him was Judge John Benson and all the politically correct figures who had given him such a hard time during that court session so long ago.

"Can you ever forgive me Kenneth? I'm so, so sorry. What a complete and utter ass I have been?"

"It was not your fault. You were as much a victim as I was. In fact, you are more of a victim as at least my mind was not altered by drugs."

"We declare ourselves true Scotsmen and true Britons", said Donald Morrison.

"We declare that we will work tirelessly to rebuild the ancient institutions of Scotland and restore her customs and traditions", said the former Politically Correct Prosecutor for former Mid-Region 12.

"And I personally declare myself loyal to the Christian faith", said the former Religious Enforcer of Politically Correct Doctrine.

"And I'm going to learn some real science", declared Donald Morrison. "Kenneth, I am sure I have a lot to learn from you."

The Lord Lieutenant of Dumfries and Galloway invited the Roman Catholic Archbishop of the same to read what all had agreed upon was the most appropriate passage from the Bible.

"When I saw the VTFC come into land a few weeks ago", began the Archbishop, "the first thing that came to mind was the passage from the Book of the Apocalypse".

'And I saw a new heaven and a new earth. For the first heaven and the first earth was gone, and the sea is now no more. And I John saw the holy city, the new Jerusalem, coming down out of heaven from God, prepared as a bride adorned for her husband. And I heard a great voice from the throne, saying: Behold the tabernacle of God with men, and he will dwell with them. And they shall be his people; and God himself with them shall be their God. And God shall wipe away all tears from their eyes: and death shall be no more, nor mourning, nor crying, nor sorrow shall be any more, for the former things are passed away. And he that sat on the throne, said: Behold, I make all things new.'

"Now that we have been liberated from the tyranny of Nazi Political Correctness, let us indeed make all things new, let us attempt to build the New Jerusalem here on Earth As it was in 1945, so it is in 2045, Europe is in ruins, so let the New Jerusalem arise Phoenix like from the ashes and may Europe, and indeed the whole world, never see these horrors again".

At 76, Sir Walter Scott Street, a happy family was re-united once again.

"What about your future Kenneth?" William Mackenzie asked his son. "You could have a brilliant career in politics. Number 10 is yours for the taking, I'm convinced."

"My passion is science. I really have no interest in politics."

"Yet no-one more than you saved this planet from Nazism and political correctness", said Morag his mother.

"But I also contributed to saving it from a 50,000 year long ice age. Mum, Dad, I was only ever political because political correctness was thrust upon me. I became a politician by default. Now I want to devote myself to science."

"What will you do now?" William asked.

"I'd like to return to Kings College University in Halifax to continue my doctoral studies. If possible, I'd like to pick up where I left off."

There was then a ring on the door-bell. William answered it. He came back into the sitting-room carrying a sealed letter. "It's for you Ken."

Kenneth tore open the envelope and read the note. "It says 'would you and Hilary please come to Bruce's Cave tomorrow afternoon at 2pm'. But Hilary is in Halifax."

"Who is asking you to go to the Cave?" Morag inquired with a worried expression on her face.

"It doesn't say".

"Be careful Kenneth", cautioned his father.

"It should be all right Dad", said Kenneth reassuringly.

"Would you like us to accompany you Kenneth?" his mother asked.

"It's very kind of you to offer but I'd better go alone in case there is any danger. But it will have to be without Hilary. Whoever wrote this note is probably unaware that Hilary is back in Canada".

Kenneth drove from Annan to Bruce's cave. He parked his car nearby and walked towards the cave entrance. As he was approaching the cave he heard footsteps behind him. He wheeled round. It was Hilary. She looked terrified.

"Hilary! How did you get here?"

"I don't know. I stepped out of the front door of my house in Halifax and here I was. But Kenneth, where am I? What is going on?"

Kenneth then proceeded to explain to Hilary all about his previous experiences inside the mysterious cave of King Robert the Bruce of Scotland.

CHAPTER 18.

Inside The Cave Again.

Kenneth and Hilary approached the entrance to the cave. Once again, the cave became mysteriously transformed into a massive seemingly endless cavern. There before them stood Black Douglas.

"Follow me, please", the Douglas commanded.

Kenneth and Hilary obeyed the summons. They followed their knightly leader through the massive cavern of burning torches, through the cavern of heraldry, past the burial vaults of Scotland's nobility and straight to the throne enclave. Robert the Bruce was waiting for them. He was already seated on the throne. The King was wearing a crown and held a golden orb in one hand a sceptre in the other.

Kenneth grabbed Hilary's hand. He saw that she was shaking. "Don't worry Hilary", he whispered to her. "We are with very good people."

Kenneth and Hilary bowed low to King Robert. From the entranceways on either side of the throne which led to the great dining hall, figures proceeded forth. From the entranceway on King Robert's right came William Wallace and Rob Roy Macgregor. From the entranceway on the left of the King came Sir Walter Scott and Robert Burns.

"We met before", said Rob Roy.

"Do you remember us?" asked Wallace.

"I remember all of you. But my fiancé Hilary does not know you?"

On King Robert's command, Kenneth introduced the four newcomers to Hilary.

"Now said King Robert", stepping off his throne, "come with us and know us better."

Kenneth and Hilary followed their ghostly companions through an opening on the left wall. It was one that Kenneth had not noticed before. When they emerged on the other side, they were aghast to find themselves once more in Radiant City on Mars!

King Robert turned around and revealed the face of Stephen Latimore. Black Douglas turned around and Kenneth and Hilary beheld the countenance of Tony Kent, the Halifax Police Chief. William Wallace transformed into Dr. Rudolph Von Hildeger and Rob Roy became Dr. Wilhelm Shneiderer. Robert Burns turned out to be David Wilson and Sir Walter Scott was none other than Gustaf Krobels.

Kenneth and Hilary were dumbfounded. They simply stood agape. The six men smiled kindly upon their two guests.

"So you were impersonating the great heroes of Scotland", Kenneth blurted out.

"No Kenneth", said Stephen Latimore. "The impersonations are what you see now".

"But wait", said Hilary. "Didn't you Herr Krobels come up with the ridiculous idea of legislation against the dust particles?"

"Yes of course", answered Krobels casually. "It was a way of diverting attention while we got on with the military preparations".

"How come we are on Mars?" Kenneth asked.

"You are a scientist Kenneth", answered Tony Kent. "But science has yet to even scratch the surface of the vast, unknown and mysterious dimensions of time and space".

"Do you remember how astonished you were Kenneth when, on your first trip to Mars, I addressed you as 'Sir Kenneth'?" Von Hildeger asked. "You were amazed at how we all knew about your experiences in the cave."

" Well", said Kenneth, "my question has now been satisfactorily answered, but why did you not bring me to Mars by this method during the first trip?"

"Kenneth", said Wilhelm Shneiderer, "the time was not yet ripe. Things must be done in stages".

"May I ask why you have brought us here again", Hilary asked.

"We want to give you a grand tour of all of the underground cities on Mars", David Wilson answered.

"But why?" continued Hilary with her queries.

"Because they will never be seen again".

"Whatever do you mean?" said Kenneth somewhat startled.

No answer was given. "The tour will take about one month", said Tony Kent.

"But our folks back on Earth will be worried about us", objected Hilary.

"They won't even know you've been gone", said Latimore.

One month later, Kenneth and Hilary were ready to return home. He was carrying a large case of computer software which his friends had given him.

"What you have there Kenneth, will keep you in post-doctoral research for the rest of your life", said Von Hildeger. What Kenneth had been given was the entire blue-print for Martian style underground cities. The computer software contained all the science and technological developments that the Mars colonies had developed over the past 100 years.

"When you have deciphered these Kenneth", said Kent, "the Earth will be a vastly different place".

"But a better place", commented Kenneth.

"As long as they don't get into the wrong hands", warned Shneiderer.

"We trust to your great prudence and judgement Kenneth", said Latimore.

The eight friends were standing outside the expensive restaurant to which Kenneth had been brought when he was first taken to Mars.

"Let us enter and have a final farewell dinner before we part forever on this side of eternity", said Gustaf Krobels.

When they went through the door they found that instead of being in the restaurant, they were in the great dining hall of the cave. Their six friends were once more the famous personages of Scotland's yesteryear. With the nobility of Scotland, they sat down to a sumptuous royal feast of venison, swan, goose and beef. Jesters tumbled, jugglers juggled and troubadours sang their love songs and ballads. It was everything a medieval banquet had to offer. Not only was the food and wine of the finest quality, but the laughter and merriment could have cheered the most miserable soul in hell.

When the banquet was over, King Robert and his entourage with their two guests entered the throne room once more. King Robert sat upon the throne and imparted his kingly blessings upon his two guests. "Go in peace and may God be always with you", was his final parting words. Black Douglas led Kenneth and Hilary through the great cavern to the simple cave entrance. When Kenneth and his fiancé exited the cave, Black Douglas had disappeared.

Kenneth looked at his watch – it was still only 2pm on August 20th 2045, the very day and time when he and Hilary had entered the cave!

That same evening, when the stars came out, Kenneth and Hilary were romantically walking hand-in-hand in the countryside around Annan. They looked up and saw the red planet shining so prominently in all its glory.

"Was it all a dream Ken?" asked Hilary sleepily. "Did it all really happen?"

"What are dreams, what is reality?" said Kenneth philosophically. "Perhaps it was all a dream – a figment of our imagination".

"But the horrors of Political Correctness were real enough."

"Really", Kenneth laughed. "That's the most unreal thing that ever happened to mankind."

Twenty years later the horrors of PCism and the final conflict with the Nazis were fast fading from peoples' minds. Kenneth, Hilary and their two teenage children were walking under a starry night sky. They concentrated their gaze upon Mars and once more became deeply thoughtful. Kenneth had designed the VSPCs for interplanetary travel and exploration according to the designs he had been given on his last visit to Mars. So much had been discovered as the solar system started to reveal more and more of its secrets, but the glass worms and the cities on Mars had completely disappeared. Radio transmissions proved to be futile and even manned missions found nothing but a barren, cold and lifeless planet.

"What are the glass tubes and cities on Mars?" asked one of the children

"And what is Political Correctness?" asked the other. "And Nazism?"

"And how do Political Correctness and Nazism connect?"

"And what have they to do with glass tubes on Mars?"

"Yes, and how would Robert the Bruce and other famous Scottish notables tie in with these? They are so distant in time and space".

"Ah – time and space", sighed their father. "Time and space", he repeated heaving out another sigh.

"So where do time and space come in?" asked one of the children.

Their mother and father smiled lovingly on their children. "Believe me", said their mother, "it's so much better that you don't know, for we ourselves are still trying to piece it all together."

EPILOGUE.

The Holy City Hymn

Last night I lay a-sleeping
There came a dream so fair,
I stood in old Jerusalem
Beside the temple there.
I heard the children singing,
And ever as they sang,
Me thought the voice of angels
From heaven in answer rang.

Jerusalem! Jerusalem!
Lift up your gates and sing,
Hosanna in the highest!
Hosanna to your King!

And then me thought my dream was changed,
The streets no longer rang,
Hushed were the glad Hosannas
The little children sang.
The sun grew dark with mystery,
The morn was cold and chill,
As the shadow of a cross arose
Upon a lonely hill.

Jerusalem! Jerusalem!
Hark! How the angels sing,
Hosanna in the highest!
Hosanna to your King!

And once again the scene was changed;
New earth there seemed to be;
I saw the Holy City
Beside the tideless sea;
The light of God was on its streets,
The gates were open wide,
And all who would might enter,
And no one was denied.
No need of moon or stars by night,
Or sun to shine by day;
It was the new Jerusalem
That would not pass away.

Jerusalem! Jerusalem!
Sing for the night is o'er!
Hosanna in the highest!
Hosanna for evermore

www.ingramcontent.com/pod-product-compliance
Lightning Source LLC
Chambersburg PA
CBHW050804250626
47155CB00005B/2199

9781426927805